ONE SERIOUSLY MESSED-UP WEEK-END IN THE OTHERWISE UN-MESSED-UP life of (JACK) SAMSONITE

BY TOM CLEMPSON

One Seriously Messed-Up Week

TOM CLEMPSON

ONE SERIOUSLY MESSED-UP WEEK-END IN THE OTHERWISE UN-MESSED-UP life of JACK SAMSONITE

www.atombooks.net

ATOM

First published in Great Britain in 2013 by Atom

A CIP catalogue record for this book
is available from the British Library.

ISBN 978-1-907411-69-4

Typeset in Melior by M Rules
Printed and bound in Great Britain by
Clays Ltd, St Ives plc

Papers used by Atom are from well-managed forests
and other responsible sources.

MIX
Paper from
responsible sources
FSC® C104740

Atom
An imprint of
Little, Brown Book Group
100 Victoria Embankment
London EC4Y 0DY

An Hachette UK Company
www.hachette.co.uk

www.atombooks.net

For my brother Joss, who died courageously
chasing fighter jets in his kitchen.
We love you always.
(Sorry this is no masterpiece and for dedicating
a story to you which, let's face it, mostly centres around
poo-trousers but, hey, it's the best I could do at the time!)
1975 – 2011

ONE SERIOUSLY MESSED–UP WEEK*END*

In the Otherwise Un-messed-up Life
of Jack Samsonite

(not including this one other time,
which was also totally messed-up, where loads of
mental stuff happened, which was quite similar to this,
but also not, and probably not really worth mentioning,
and now I'm thinking that I should maybe have just
left the title as 'One Seriously Messed-Up Weekend'
and not bothered with all this extra stuff, because
now it just seems confusing, and messy, and like
I'm a bit of an idiot and ...)

MORNING: WALKING
TO SCHOOL

'We need to do something cool,' I announced.

'What?' James asked.

'We need to do something really cool,' I repeated (only this time I added the word 'really').

'I heard what you said. What cool thing do we need to do?'

'I don't know. Something really cool and really big and right now.'

'Why?'

'Because I'm writing a film,' I explained.

'A film about what?'

'Us.'

'Don't be a twat.'

'I'm serious!'

'Shut up now, please.'

'Why?'

'Because you're annoying me.'

'Tough. We need to do something really ...'

'Why are you holding your phone like that?' James interrupted.

'Because I'm recording us.'

'Why?'

'So I don't have to write down everything we're saying.'

'Why would you want to write down everything we're saying?'

'I don't, that's why I'm recording it.'

'You're a twat.'

'I know. Please can we just do something really cool before it's too la—'

It's too late.

Enter Tim – small, irritating hanger-on – the one thing guaranteed to prevent anything cool from ever happening. Ever.

'Hello, Mr Little Willy! Hello, Mr Littler Willy!' Tim greeted us in an annoyingly bouncy way.

'Why am I Mr Littler Willy?' James protested.

'What you doing with your phone?' Tim asked.

'Writing a film,' I explained.

'Oh, right, cool. Did you see *Dr Who* last night?'

'Who says mine's smaller than Jack's?' demanded James.

'Don't start talking about *Dr Who*, Tim – we're trying to do something cool here,' I pleaded.

'If your life was a film, who would do the voiceover?' Tim asked, obediently changing the subject.

'Morgan Freeman,' James answered without a moment's hesitation. 'Morgan Freeman should do the voiceover for everything.'

'Did you know his name is an anagram of Frogman Reeman?' Tim blurted.

'Guyyyys!' I whined. 'Please!'

'James was a quiet young man,' James said, doing a crap impersonation of Morgan Freeman. 'He kept himself to himself, stayed out of trouble, had a larger than average willy ...'

'I said *something cool*!' I reminded them.

'Just don't go around calling me Mr Little Willy, please, Tim,' James muttered. Then, 'Don't step in the poo!'

'Come on, guys,' I pleaded again. 'I want the beginning to be one of those openings that really blows you away, like a big blockbuster movie, like the title shoots up onto the screen ... *Jack* – BAM! *Samsonite* – BAM! *The Movie* – BOOM!'

'You've got shit on your shoe,' said James.

'If you had to kiss a guy, who would it be?' asked Tim.

'Guys! I mean, *really* cool! Like, "That was the best beginning to anything. EVER!"'

'You're scuffing shit all up your trouser leg, Jack.'

'Oh, shit!' roared Tim, bursting into idiot-laughter. 'You're covered in dog crap!'

'And you've sat in gum or something,' added James.

'What?'

'And your flies are undone ...'

JACK

(BAM!)

SAMSONITE

(BAM!)

THE MOVIE

(boom)

THIS IS ME

Most people in the world are Hollywood blockbusters. They are clean, shiny, formulaic, life-by-numbers, clones of previous successes that they are trying to rip off. They all have these big-budget, glossy, life-defining plans: 'I'm going to study *this* ... I'm going to marry *her* ... I'm going to live *here* and do *this* career ... I like *this* type of music, *this* type of girl, *this* kind of cheese on *this* make of bread, and I do *this* many poos at *these* times of the day ... ' They tick all the right boxes, follow all the right rules, and always do the right thing. I am so indescribably envious of these people – the people with plans, the people who have made their minds up about everything. I hate them. I want to be one of them.

I haven't made my mind up about *anything*. I am a low-budget, experimental, euro-arthouse, open-ended, doesn't-make-much-sense, don't-think-I'd-watch-it-twice box-office flop. I need focus. I need direction. I need to make decisions. And time is running out.

Pick a college.   Pick a career.

          Pick a girl.   Pick a government.

                    Pick a toilet.

Pick a personality.

          Pick a frickin' ... I don't know, but LOTS of things!

Something has to change, because now is decision time.

1. I *need* to pick a girl. I'm seventeen. I'm still a
    virgin. In a few months, I will be leaving school
    for ever, and all the girls I know will be gone. I'll
    have to start all over again, from square one,
    with *strangers*! Eight years of meticulously
    plotted wooing will be down the drain.
2. I *need* to pick a career, so that I can pick a
    course, so that I can pick a university. Do I want
    to be a film-maker or a writer? The deadline for
    sending applications is next Monday. Today is
    Thursday.
3. I need to write my Personal Statement for said
    application. That doesn't sound very difficult,
    right? Wrong. It's impossible. Trust me, I've
    tried. Over and over and over again. Every
    sentence I write seems to begin with 'I': *'I'm a
    hard worker ... I'm a dedicated student ... I
    enjoy making films ... I like to socialise ... I'm*

a complete spod.' So far, I have written eight different Personal Statements. All of them suck. How am I supposed to explain who I am to someone else, in just two pages, without making myself sound like a twat? My current opinion on that is this: I can't. So, I've decided, if I want to avoid messy, fumbling, stumbling, stupid, twatty me-ness, then I am going to live my life like a Hollywood blockbuster. We all want our lives to be more like the movies, so I'm going to try to make that a reality. I'm going to be a hero. I'm going to create an alter-ego. I'm going to become ... JackMan.

The new, cooler, sexier, more confident me, starts *nnnnnnnnn* ... now.

JACK SAMSONITE: THE MOVIE

EXT. SCHOOL FORECOURT — DAY

SMASH CUT:
BAM! Three guys strut coolly, in the bright
morning sun, towards the school entrance. Slow
motion. Awesome music pumps loudly from
somewhere. All the chicks are checking them
out. They're lapping up the attention. These
are clearly the No. 1 dudes.

CRASH ZOOM on Guy #1.
Freeze frame.
His bio slams onto the screen.

  Name: Jack 'The Killer' Samsonite
  Age: 17
  Profession: Assassin
  Civilian Alter-ego: School kid
  Motto: "I do what I gotta do."
  Status: The No.1 Dude

Un-freeze. They do something really cool or
something.
Freeze frame on guy #2.

  Name: James 'Mr Littler Willy' Krippin
  Age: 17
  Profession: Explosives expert

Motto: "I blow shit up."
Status: 2nd in command

Un-freeze. They do more really, really cool
stuff that's also really, really cool.
Freeze frame on guy #3.

Name: Tim 'The Annoying Little Tit'
Suchton
Age: 17
Mental Age: 7
Profession: Idiot
Motto: "I just wiped my bum, but it was
all kind of soggy, and the paper ripped in
the middle, and I got poo on my finger."
Status: Accidental friend

The screen bursts back into motion. The trio
reach the school steps. Guy #1 (Jack) senses
danger. Some doof falls off his skateboard and
the board comes rocketing towards our trio.
People gasp in fear. Tim dives out of the way.
James ducks for cover. But Jack isn't fazed.
He effortlessly halts the skateboard with his
foot, flips it into the air, jumps on board,
perfects a 360-degree ollie fakie, then rolls
through the school doors.

The girls gasp again. But, this time, not in
fear ... in complete fanny-melting lust.

IN SCHOOL

'Why the hell did you just try to ride that kid's skateboard?' asked James, whilst I hobbled in through the entrance doors, clutching my knee and trying not to cry. 'You can't skate to save your life! Why would you do that?'

The chorus of laughter that followed me into the entrance hall assured me that nothing had changed. Even though I am now in Year 13 – the final year of sixth form, the most respected position in school – I am still just me. Hapless, talentless, loser me. Twat me. Nothing will ever change that. You know how, after every school holiday, you have this stupid fantasy about turning up to school in brand-new clothes, awesome new haircut and a body so ripped you make [insert name of most ripped person you know here] look like a prima ballerina? And you know how when you do actually turn up at school on your first day back, you've actually grown a bunch of spots on your face, accidentally eaten fourteen too many pizzas over the past six weeks, your bad hair day makes you look like you hire your mum as your barber, and your shit clothes are made even shitter by the fact that you trod dog crap up your trouser leg and your flies keep dropping down? Well, that didn't happen to James. He really was one of those loathsome wankers who turned up five inches taller, six abs buffer, hair like a movie star and with a tan that perfectly matched his parents' over-priced three-week holiday to the Bahamas. It was horrible. The small, geeky, nobody boy who used to think I walked on water had suddenly become a towering, hulky, ladies' man; one who now thinks the only water I walk on comes in the form of puddles in front of the toilet.

Change of plan. My screenplay character will no longer be a cool assassin (I'm not too sure I can make that believable). He's now going to be a super-cool fanny-magnet. I can do that. I *will* do that. I have to do that, or I'm just going to look like second best. Plus, I suppose, if I'm writing an *improvement* of my life, it should probably be slightly less completely made-up. And, if I want to be able to use the finished screenplay to go in my portfolio, to help me get into a university, I should probably try to make it slightly less completely crap. So, I'll have to pick the coolest, most interesting elements of my life and write about those instead.

There's just one problem . . .

MY LIFE IS AS COOL AND INTERESTING AS AN OLD MAN'S SWEATY BALL-BAG

(This may also be my Personal Statement downfall.)

MY LIFE SUMMED UP

My life is pretty easy to sum up. It goes something like this ...

BLERRRRRRRRRRRRRRRRRGGGGGGHHHHHHHHHHH-HHHH . . . .

No, seriously, look:

Age: 0 to 14. Interesting things that happened = nothing.

Age: 15 years, 11 months and 2 weeks to 15 years, 11 months, 3 weeks. Interesting things that happened = changed my name, got hunted down by a mentalist, got my heart blown into a million pieces, fell out of love, fell in love, got hit in the head lots, tried to blackmail someone, got betrayed by everyone, saw some girls in their undies, learned the true dangers of banana skins, got hit in the head some more, nearly died, a girl cupped my nuts.*

---

* For more information on all this, please see 'One Seriously Messed-Up Week in the Otherwise Mundane and Uneventful Life of Jack Samsonite' published by Sweaty Teenage Loser Publications, available in all good second-drawer-down of my bedside tables.

Age: 15 years, 11 months, 3 weeks to present day. Interesting things that happened = learned that girls are completely unpredictable and mental, and that nut-cupping does not equal love. Learned that blackmail gets you nowhere (especially when you're bluffing). Failed to get into decent college (which explains why I stayed on for sixth form). And, also, the most prominent occurrence: a huge big pile of nothing.

OK, so, yeah, two years ago there was one week of crazy mental stuff. Every week since then? Boring, dull, monotonous, mundane nothing.

In fact, the incident that occurred just five minutes ago sums my life up pretty well . . .

I'd been in the main school toilets, attempting to wash dog crap off my combat trousers, and was running late for registration (if you miss registration they mark you as being absent for the whole day), so I took the shortest route from the main school toilets to the sixth-form block (we have our own building now we're in the sixth form). That's what all smart people in a rush would do, right? Take the shortest route possible? Nuh-uh. Because a *smart* person in a rush would have remembered that the shortest route runs between the outside wall of the school, and the two Portaclassrooms (basically, large prefabricated sheds that the school brought in when they started running out of room), which are home to the Year 7s From Hell.

Now, I'm pretty sure that when I was in Year 7 I was:

a) NEVER as small as these new kids and, more importantly . . .

b) A lot more respectful (and fearful) of the sixth formers.

Not these tiny shits from hell, though. For they are both tiny ... and shits from hell.

By the time I'd realised my mistake it was already too late. I was directly outside The Cabin At The Edge Of The School. I know I shouldn't feel intimidated by these midget demons: no other self-respecting sixth former would get scared by a bunch of kids straight out of baby school. I am seventeen years old for Christ's sake! I'm old enough to work, drive, get married, raise a family, win the lottery, have sex with a consenting adult ...

Man, that is really depressing. I've been legally allowed to go shagging for over a year now, yet I still haven't even kissed a girl on the mouth yet! Did you hear me? I am SEVENTEEN and I am still a *kiss* virgin!

All of a sudden, I have realised what needs to happen in my film/life.

JACK SAMSONITE: THE MOVIE

EXT. SCHOOL — DAY

Our hero saunters nonchalantly past the hut
where the Pygmy Warriors of the Wank-face
tribe are known to reside. He doesn't seem to
care. All he cares about is kissing girls.
That's what he does, you see. He's a girl
kisser. A super-bad, mother-lovin', ball-
breaker of a girl kisser.

Then, just as he is remembering the last hot
girl that he kissed (which was only two
minutes ago, and she was really, really
hot) ... BOOM! All the windows and doors of the
hut suddenly burst open, and our hero is
thrown into action.

Freeze frame.
His bio bursts onto screen.

Name: Jack 'The Kisser' Samsonite
Profession: Girl kisser (on the lips, and
you better believe it!)
Motto: "I do what I gotta do."
Status: The No.1 Dude Kisser (actually,
no, that makes it sound like I kiss dudes,
doesn't it? Let's try ...)
The No.1 Kissing Dude (better? Or does it
sound like I kiss number ones? Wee-wee.

Like, The Urine Kissing Dude? That would
be bad. They'd call me Piss-lips and
stuff. No. Maybe I should just stick
to ...)
The No.1 Dude (or does that make me sound
like 'The Wee-wee boy'? Oh, whatever, who
cares ...)

The screen explodes back into action and the
Wank-face Pygmy Warriors are on full attack ...

THE BATTLE: ONE MAN vs AN ENTIRE ARMY

'Oy! Gay boy, lend us five quid!' came the first, near-lethal blow from the Pygmies' leader, dangling out of one of the hut windows.

I did my best to quell my nerves, steady my trembling hands, loosen my tense and seizing joints, and somehow managed to counter-attack with an eye-wateringly sharp come-back: 'No,' I meekly mumbled, carefully avoiding eye contact.

Ha! That'll teach 'em!

'Hey, mate, you a teacher?' another Pygmy Wank-face asked.

'He's not a teacher, you twat!' laughed the Pygmy leader. 'He's a gay-boy from my bus!'

'Is he gay? Hey, mate, you a shit-stabber?'

Also, I'm fairly certain I was never this homophobic in Year 7, either. Idiots. I didn't answer. I continued walking, and focused all my energy on not looking scared. I'm guessing I failed because ...

'Why are you so red?' a gum-chewing Pygmy pig-faced girl asked.

''Cos he fancies you!' the second Pygmy Wank-face laughed.

'Ergh!' she protested, spitting her gum at my feet. 'Sick!'

'He don't fancy *her*!' the Pygmy leader yelled in an accent known as fake-cockney (or Mockney), which he affected to make himself seem rougher than his middle-class upbringing might suggest. 'He's gay, ain't he! He fancies *you*!'

'Euuurrrrrgghhhhhh!' They all laughed and jeered.

'That true?' the gum-chewing Pygmy pig-faced girl asked. 'You fancy Vince?'

'Noooo,' I sighed, wishing it wouldn't be unacceptable for me to run away.

'What you hanging around outside our form room for, then?' she challenged.

I had to show them I wasn't weak. If they smelled my fear they'd annihilate me. But I also had to remain calm. If they knew they were getting to me they would make this a regular sport, following me around school – like what happened with Evan Holding in the year below (who, thanks to Year 7s, is now known as 'Granny Shagger'). I chose my response very carefully, and simply shot them a lazy, but highly serious, don't-mess-with-me glare.

'Ergh! Did you see that?' reeled the second Pygmy Wankface. 'He looked at me!'

'What you looking at him for?'

'Are you a paedophile?!'

'Someone get Miss Harding. Paedophile on the loose!'

'Miss! Miss! This man's looking at Vincent!'

'He tried to touch him!'

'And his flies are undone!'

21

A balled-up piece of paper ricocheted off my ear before I finally made it out into the open. I had cleared the hut. I was safe. I had survived ... this time. But I may not be so lucky next time. That's why I had better make sure there is no next time.

Always take the long route. Always! How could I have been so stupid? I could have died!

From now on, everything I do has to be carefully considered and calculated. I'm the star of a film now. I can't just go around making stupid mistakes. *I need to be the hero. I need to stop trembling before I get into registration. I need something to take my mind off my recent brush with death.*

And then I saw her.

And, all of a sudden, my life found focus.

REGISTRATION (WITH 'HER')

I'd heard all about 'her'. She recently moved next door to Tim, and, thanks to his serial-killer-style obsession with 'her', I now know exactly what music she listens to, what time of day she showers, what incense she burns in her bedroom and what it smells like on Tim's pillow when he has left his window open to soak up as much of her as possible.

Yes, she has inspired Tim to be a complete nut-job. He has even started wearing skinny, purple, semi-flared corduroy trousers in an attempt at being as hippy-ish as her, in a hope that it will make her fall instantly in love with him. SKINNY PURPLE CORDUROY FLARES! This is exactly the type of clothing Tim would usually laugh at if he saw it on other people!

So, yes, I knew a lot about her daily habits. But what I didn't know was her name, what she was doing at our school, or that she really was every bit as hot as Tim had described her to be. And more.

OK, if I'm going to be honest, I didn't just see 'her': I saw 'her' and '*her*'. But I have to learn to forget about '*her*'. She's totally beautiful and everything, but she's made it clear that nothing can happen between us. There was a time, a few years ago – when we were best friends – that I asked her to hold my balls for me, and then it all went weird and she became really distant. I don't know why. I'm guessing it's got something to do with the fact that she's a girl, and girls are TOTALLY FRICKIN' MENTAL. (I'm hoping that the girl walking into the sixth-form block with '*her*' is slightly less mental though, because I totally want to kiss her on the mouth.)

I know this whole 'I've gotta lose my virginity before the end of the film' is really clichéd and everyone thinks it's all boys ever think about, and we're all the same, and it's, like, the motivation for the characters in almost every teen movie ever made, but seriously, hear me out . . . Think about it like this: you've been waiting your whole life to try this one chocolate bar. You've heard all about how amazing this chocolate bar is – it's REALLY amazing – I mean, people won't shut up about it, but you're not legally allowed to eat it (OK, so you've come across a few stray bars of this chocolate hanging around from time to time, and one of them might come up to you and say, '*My mate thinks you're OK, and wants to know if you want to eat her face,*' but you're too scared and intimidated, so you use the whole 'law' thing as a good excuse for not doing it), but then the day comes and they say, 'You are now of age. You have our permission to eat the world's most amazing chocolate. Go forth, and eat to your heart's content.' And all of a sudden you're like, 'Ummm, all right, but . . . well . . . I . . . what if the chocolate rejects me and laughs at my willy?'

So that's why I'm taking baby steps. First snog before first shag. It's just the way of the world. You've got to learn to walk before you can run. Or is it learn to crawl before you can walk? Or is it crawl and run? I dunno. It doesn't matter. You get what I mean.

Anyway, as I walked into the sixth-form common room for registration, I saw 'her' (sitting next to '*her*'), and I knew I had to make my next move count. I had to make the perfect first impression. So I did what I do best. I sat in a corner and buried my face in my notebook.

But sooner or later I knew I was going to meet her. I was going to *talk* to her. I was going to make my ever-lasting first impression.

Unfortunately, it happened a little sooner than I was prepared for.

FIRST IMPRESSIONS

Everything about this girl made my head hurt. I know the opposite sex is supposed to be difficult to figure out, but she was something else.

Why is she starting our sixth form when we're so close to leaving school for ever?

Why is she so damn hot?

How does she know 'her'?

Why am I attracted to someone who is so not my type?

OK, I didn't actually think I had a type until that last thought. In fact, I've actively *avoided* having a type. It's hard enough getting a girlfriend as it is, without having to make sure they measure up to any rigorous checklist. And, as each girlfriendless year passes, my standards have lowered, until ... I've accidentally created a 'type' for myself.

MY (accidental) TYPE

1. **They mustn't spend all week bragging about who they shagged at the weekend**
2. **They mustn't be better looking than me**
3. **They mustn't scare me in any way whatsoever.**

Unfortunately, this checklist has limited me to one girl in our sixth form: Mimi 'Mouse' Burke. She is very small (like a mouse); she is very shy (like a mouse); and instead of talking she just kind of squeaks (like a mouse). Plus she looks like a mouse. Actually, forget it, she is so mouse-like she actually violates point 3 on the checklist. And this new girl – 'her' – *definitely* violates point 2, which in turn violates point 3 and, even if she doesn't spend all week talking about it, I imagine a girl like her can get sex on demand.

I know I have no chance with 'her' in the slightest. Unless she happens to be one of those weird beautiful girls who are attracted to big freaky losers, or I can manage to trick her into thinking I'm far more impressive than I actually am (not like Superman does to Lois Lane, making her think he's totally a different person: a mumbling, bumbling, weedy fool instead of the man of steel. Tosser!). No, maybe I'll still be me, but I'll just be the best bits of me, and less of the crap bits. The—

'Jack!'

I looked up. It was '*her*' (not 'her', try to keep up). She was beckoning me over. My time was up.

I'm going in.

AND THIS IS WHAT I SAID

I got up out of my seat. I was on autopilot: I didn't know what I was doing. I just started moving. Em ('*her*') had said 'come', so I went. My heart was pounding, my head was floating, and my feet were doing their own little thing.

This is it. I have a whole new opportunity. I can start fresh with '*her*' *because she doesn't know I'm a loser ... she's new.*

It was no use. She was going to hate me any way. These kinds of girls always do.

I can at least try to make a good first impression.

Good first impressions *are* good. Except ...

Crap! I'm weird, funny-looking and I smell like dog poo!

Bad first impressions are bad.

I'm not *weird and funny-looking,* I tried to convince myself. (There was nothing I could do about the dog poo right then.)

I'm not weird and funny-looking! I insisted, with little success.

My name is Jack Samsonite, and I am super-cool.

Better.

My name is Jack Samsonite and I am super-cool!

It was working. *Keep it up!*

My name is Jack Samsonite and I am su-per-cool!

Yes!

I am super-cool! And she is super-hot! We must cuddle!

Hell, yeah!

My name is Jack Samsonite and I am puser-cool!

No! *Ignore her hotness! Remain suser-cool!*

Noooo. Crap!

My name I Sack Jam ...

NO!

'Hey, buddy,' smiled Em as I approached their table. 'This is Edith.'

Edith smiled and wiggled her fingers. 'And you are ...?' she prompted.

My name is Jack Samsonite and ...

'I am puper ...'

NOOOOO!!

Em doubled over as a huge laugh exploded from her mouth. 'Hey! Pooper!' she laughed. 'I had a grandad called Pooper!'

'I didn't mean to say "Pooper",' I explained, with an annoyingly nervous through-the-teeth laugh.

'No?' Edith said, in mock surprise.

'Ignore me,' I said with a blush. 'I'm a retard.'

And that's when everybody stopped laughing.

'That's not very funny,' Edith said, coldly.

Oh.

'No, I ...'

Explain!

'My big brother has LIC,' she informed me.

29

'Oh ... I ...'

What the hell is LIC?

'Sorry,' I stuttered, 'I was just ...'

Rewind.

Please god.

REWIND!!

JACK SAMSONITE'S PERSONAL STATEMENT: ATTEMPT #9

My name is Jack Samsonite. I am a socially inept, romantically dysfunctional, potty-mouthed tosser and COMPLETE FRICKING IDIOT! I would greatly appreciate you considering me to be a part of your university.

JACK SAMSONITE: THE MOVIE

INT. EMPTY CLASSROOM — DAY

Jack is working hard, writing genius stuff in
his notebook, when the door quietly swings
open behind him.

VOICE

You and I need to have words.

Startled, Jack spins in his chair to see a
very stern-looking Edith standing in the
doorway, glowering at him.

JACK

I ...

EDITH

I don't want to hear it, Samsonite.

JACK

I didn't mean to ...

EDITH

I said, shut your mouth, bitch!

Edith marches across the room. She clasps a
hand around Jack's throat and presses her knee
into his groin.

                    EDITH (growling)
That word you used ...

                    JACK
Honestly, I really am ...

                    EDITH
I don't like that word.

Edith moves her face towards Jack's until
they are just an inch apart. She glances down
at his crotch, then she moves in for the
kill.

Freeze frame.
Her bio slams onto the screen.

BAM!

    NAME: Edith Wow *[must find out her surname]*
    AGE: Nice
    SEX: Hell yeah
    PROFESSION: Hot
    STATUS: Ummm ... hot?
    MOTTO: 'I'm hot, and I think you're hot
    too, and together we can be two hot
    people, getting it on, and getting really,
    really hot.'
    COMPATIBILITY CHECK: [Scrolling text with
    accompanying VOICEOVER]

                      33

PROS

- She actually exists in the real world, unlike other people of her calibre who only seem to exist in movies or on magazine covers. This may be my only opportunity to ever converse with someone this hot!

- She is a hippy (or, at least, she dresses like one), and hippies are naturally open-minded and like to focus on inner beauty (or at least that's what I like to believe), so there's a chance she might look beyond my camp T-shirts, my special hair cut, my spotty forehead, my semi-moobs, my small willy, my dog-poo trousers, my ... I may as well just smash a spade into my face, wear a 'I Hate Retards' T-shirt and call myself 'Nancy'. I don't stand a hope in hell.

CONS

- For her to go out with me would be as likely as the Mir Space Station just nipping back to earth to refuel at the little garage in the village next to mine.
- I said the word 'retard' in front of her.
- She hates me and thinks I'm a bigoted twat.
- Tim is obsessed with her. He'd probably sneak into my house and castrate me in my sleep if I so much as wink at her toes!
- She's hot. I'm not.

THE OTHER FILM

Sometimes things happen in your life that are so EARTH-SHATTERINGLY HUGE that, all of a sudden, they make the rest of your life seem tiny and unimportant by comparison. I know this because I've read about it: near-death experience, having your first child, terminal illness, sudden unemployment – these are some of the most common causes. Now add to that list: insulting a hot girl with an LIC brother by saying 'retard'. That's why, when it came to meeting Ben Marshall (the media studies teacher) during our study period, to discuss my final project – a short film (the connecting piece in my foolproof university application triple whammy, the success of which will dictate the trajectory of my future career and the rest of my life) – I didn't really care any more.

Luckily, he kept it brief.

'I like the idea, Jarrod,' he told me.

'That's good,' I replied.

'It is good, Jarrod.'

'Good.'

'But ...'

'But?'

'The title.'

'Oh.'

'Yes.'

'Not good?'

'Not good, Jarrod. You just can't.'

'I didn't think we could.'

'Not a good idea.'

'Wasn't my idea.'

'Change the title.'

'Yes.'

'Also . . .'

'Yes?'

'It needs a love interest.'

HA! EASY!

'Done.'

'And . . .'

'And?'

'A villain.'

'Love interest. Check. Villains. Check.'

'Not check, Jarrod. Vill*ain*. Not villain*s*. Don't make the superhero movie error of adding too many villains. Too messy. Big mistake.'

'OK.'

'Be brave. Be original.'

'Brave. Original. Stick to the superhero formula. Got it.'

'And we're done.'

And we *were* done. I can't say I agreed with everything he said (in fact, a lot of what he said made no sense to me whatsoever), but he is the man who will be marking this film, and, unlike my GCSEs, I WILL get a good grade and I WILL get into film school. So, as long as he is happy, I am happy.

I'm just not sure the rest of my group will agree.

CHANGE OF PLAN

'Offensive *how*?' demanded Tim, who'd been anxiously waiting outside the media suite, with James, to hear Ben's verdict on our short film idea.

'Well, apparently, for some weird reason, teachers don't want to be represented as bumbling, incompetent, moronic monsters,' I explained, knowing that sarcasm would be totally wasted on Tim.

'So he thinks we're just going to change the title?' Tim complained, as we walked back towards the sixth-form block.

'We *are* going to change the title,' James told him firmly. 'Like me and Jack both said we should *two weeks ago*!'

'Yeah,' I agreed. 'Plus, *Brain-dead Idiot Zombie Teachers From Hell* doesn't really work as a title for a superhero film.' Then I winced, knowing what was coming.

'A super-*what*?' snarled Tim.

'What superhero film?' James asked, puzzled.

'Ummm ... we're kind of changing the story a little bit ... of a lot.' I figured that if I dropped in that little piece of information in a nonchalant, throwaway manner, they might not make a big deal of it.

'WHAT?' James and Tim roared.

'I think that maybe he might have got our idea muddled up with someone else's superhero idea, and that maybe he might think that their superhero idea is actually really good, whereas our zombie one is kind of stupid.'

'Why?' demanded Tim. 'What ... *WHY?*'

'Well,' I explained, using calming and reassuring tones, 'first of all he thinks my name is Jarrod. And, secondly, he thinks that if I play a superhero, who gets it on with a hot girl, we could maybe get quite a good grade, so ...'

'WHAT?' Tim erupted again, now in a massive toddler-type tantrum.

'But we can still film it in a documentary style!' I reassured him (doing it hand-held, *Blair Witch Project*, docu-style was something he had been really excited about, along with ...), 'and we can still film a scene on the roof!'

This seemed to calm him down a bit.

'So, you get to play the hero and you get to kiss a girl ... and what else?' asked James, who was managing to remain kind of neutral to the news.

'And we need a villain, too!' I told him, knowing he'd love to play that role.

'A villain!' Tim smiled, finally looking excited. 'You're going to have to have a *proper* fight! Who are you gonna fight?'

'Err ...'

I hadn't thought that bit through especially well.

'If you have to have a real life kiss with a real life girl then you have to have a real life fight with a real life enemy,' Tim gleefully informed me.

'Well ... actually ... I thought ... maybe James?'

'Piss off!' James grunted. 'I'm not getting punched in the face just for a film!'

'We won't *actually* fight!' I reassured him.

'Erm ... ' said Tim, looking at me like I'm an idiot. 'Yeah, you will.'

'It's *documentary* style!' James reminded me.

'Yes, it's documentary *style*,' I emphasised in turn. 'It's not actually going to be real. I'm playing a *superhero,* remember?'

'It works the same as the zombie idea, dude.' James shook his head. 'ONE thing is make-believe; everything else is real. Like *Borat*. That was the plan. We all agreed.'

'You're having a real fight!' Tim laughed.

'*And* you have to get it on with a real person. For real,' James added.

What the hell did I just do?

Why did I ...?

I'm an idiot!

This is going to be ...

'Aaaaawesome!' Tim said with a grin.

Reminder to self: Current Total of Loose Ends to Tie Up by the End of Jack Samsonite: The Movie . . .
6

1. Lose my kiss virginity (to improve my life)
2. Write my two-page Personal Statement (for uni application)
3. Choose a career/university/university course (so that I can go to uni)
4. Make a short film (for my media studies class)
5. Get it on with a girl, on camera (for my short film for media studies class. Though I'm thinking I could combine this with Loose End No.1)
6. Find a villain and fight him on camera (also for our short film for media studies class. Probably can't combine this one with Loose End No.1)

TWO BIG PROBLEMS

So, I'm playing a superhero. I can do that. That's cool. I can *play* a superhero. Easy. Jump off buildings? Bust through walls? Run through fire and outrun trains? No problem. But I also have to kiss a girl. For real. And I have to fight someone. For real. I'm not sure I can do that. In fact, history has *proven* that I can't do that. I'm only human! What do I do? In order to get a kiss on the lips, I also have to get a punch in the face. It's the ultimate Catch-22! If this coin were any more two-sided, it'd be ... a really big, cube-like coin that was really confusing!

I have a series of options before me:

1. <u>Opt out of playing the hero, get out of having to fight someone</u>. But I also get out of having to kiss someone (I know, I don't *have* to be making a film in order to kiss a girl. Guys kiss girls every day without starring in a film. But if it were to be part of the film, then I would get James and Tim's help in getting me a girl. And, judging on the last (girl-free) seventeen

years of my life, I could use all the help I can get.)

2. <u>**Take the villain out of the equation**</u>. Tell James and Tim that Ben never said we should have a villain, that it's a silly idea, that it would just complicate things. But who am I kidding? Ben *did* say we need a villain. What kind of superhero film has no villain? No villain = bad film. Bad grade. Bad uni. Bad career. Bad life.

3. <u>**Talk James and Tim into toning down the documentary style**</u>. If we make it like a normal film and get people to *act* the other roles, then I only have to have a *pretend* fight, but still get to kiss someone!

Guess which option I'm going to go with.

I talked, I urged, I suggested, I recommended, I argued, I *insisted*, but it was no use: James and Tim had their hearts set on filming it as real as possible and, unfortunately, they had some very good points.

'We don't want to make a *normal* film!' argued Tim. 'You're the one that came up with the documentary idea in the first place! *Everyone* will be making *normal* films! We want ours to stand out!'

I heard Ben's words replay in my head: 'Be brave. Be original.'

'And,' added James, 'no one in our school can act. If we rope school kids into playing all the roles, we'll end up with some unconvincing, badly acted, shoddy piece of crap. We want it to feel *real*!'

Then, they finally got to the heart of the matter.

'Look,' said James, 'if you're worried you can't get anyone to get it on with, then I'll play the main part, if you want.'

And that was it. He had hit the nail on the head – struck the ultimate nerve. He didn't say anything about being too scared to have a real fight because, as we all know, finding someone who might want to hit me will be the easiest thing in the world. But finding someone who might want to *kiss* me ... ?

Once upon a time, James's unfaltering faith in my smoothness meant that he thought I could saunter over to any girl in school, mutter *any* unintelligent crap to her, like, 'My minion eats pickled gherkins in his vestibule,' or something, and they would've wrapped their vaginas around my face before you could say, 'JackMan is super-cool.' But now, sadly, James has known me long enough to know that when I do actually pluck up the courage to talk to girls, I generally say something *way* more stupid than 'pickles' and 'vestibules', and it usually results in them wrapping nothing around my face other than a cold, blank, death-stare, followed by the words, 'Piss off, you turd-sniffing wank-bag.'

I get the horrible feeling that James thinks I couldn't get a girl to kiss me if my future depended on it.

Well, my future *does* depend on it. And I'm going to prove him wrong.

I *HAVE* TO PROVE HIM WRONG!

I *am* JackMan.

44

My new, cooler, sexier, more confident me starts
nnnnnn . . . .

(Hang on, I just have to pick my nose first . . .)

OK.

Nnnnnnnnnnn . . . .

(Let me just get my pants out of my crack . . .)

Nnnnnnnnnn . . . now.

GET 'EM OUT

When we entered the common room for our lesson I was already pissed off, for these following reasons:

1. Our lesson was supposed to be a 'study' ('study' = 'try to make girls like me') period, but someone had imposed a proper lesson on us all (without warning!) and now we were late
2. The common room is for hanging out in (and trying to make girls like me), not for lessons
3. The teacher who was taking this impromptu lesson was the new vice principal, who is part of the new fascist regime that is sweeping through the school (casual dress, out: uniforms, in. First-name basis, out: 'sir' and 'miss', in. Budgets for arty subjects, out: budgets for Nazi subjects, in. These things haven't kicked in yet, but they're on their way). OK, so I've heard he's actually a really nice guy but, in my experience, a teacher who is referred to as a 'really nice guy' is nothing but a teacher trying to make girls like him.

The first face I saw as I entered the common room was 'hers' (well, actually it was '*hers*', but I tried to ignore *her*, and moved on to the face directly next to *her*). I desperately wanted to talk to her, to explain that I don't usually say 'retard' and, when I do say it, I'm never actually talking about genuine retards, just the stupid version of normal people (you know, the type who throw things at you in the cinema), but it was too late for explanations – the lesson had already started.

'Glad you could join us,' the vice principal scoffed, as we apologised and crossed the room.

The rest of the class chuckled and I felt like throwing popcorn in their big retard faces! (In a *NICE* way! Ughhh, I'm so misunderstood!)

The class was all standing in a circle, which looked horribly like we were about to do some dumb, Year 7-style ice-breaker session.

Grrrreat.

I had my trusty notebook in my hand, so I hastily stowed it in my backpack, but then the vice principal addressed the class.

'Notebooks out for this, thank you,' he sighed.

This seemed like a weird request. Since when do you need notebooks for ice-breaker sessions? Don't they usually just consist of throwing a ball back and forth and reciting mind-numbingly dull facts about yourself? Whatever. So I took my notebook back out of my bag, and ventured forward to find myself a place in the circle. Except, as I moved away from my bag, my shoelace must have got snagged on a chair-leg or something, because I went nowhere. It was kind of embarrassing, but it wasn't a major big deal or anything. It made a big noise, people laughed some more, I went red, untangled my lace, then stood in the circle.

(The new, cooler, sexier, more confident me, starts . . . . . . *nnnn*now.)

But the laughter didn't quite stop entirely. I looked to my left. All eyes were on me. I looked to my right. All eyes were on me. There was no doubt about it – they knew something I didn't.

But not for long.

MEET PETE (he's a twat!)

'Outside please,' said Peter Farleigh, the vice principal (and a twat).

This puzzled me because he appeared to be looking in my general direction. As did everyone else.

Is this twat talking to ME?

OK, I know it seems kind of mean that I keep calling him a twat; I mean, I don't even know him yet. You probably assume that I'm writing this with hindsight (I am, it's approximately six and a half hours later), but I knew he was a twat from the very moment I laid eyes upon him – it was twat at first sight. He has the look of a Nazi daytime TV quiz-show host/bank manager about him. Yeah, I know it's wrong to judge a book by its cover and wotnot, but this particular book happened to have shit on its cover, was entitled 'One Seriously Shit Book', and had a quote on the front that read, '*A must for fans of shit!*' (so, really, at worst all you can blame me for is falsely labelling him a 'twat' instead of a 'shit').

'Outside! Please!' he repeated, like a purple-faced nob.

Who *was* he talking to?

'Now!' he barked.

Is he seriously talking to me?

The answer was 'Yes'.

He was.

He very, very was.

IN MY FACE

Peter (stupid twat) marched me out of the common room, slammed the door as hard as he could (which wasn't actually very hard at all because it was fitted with one of those self-closing mechanisms that makes it impossible to slam – ha!), then towered over me with huge, suited, overweight, red-faced, twatting fury.

Still not sure what exactly I had done wrong, I waited for him to explode in my face. But he didn't. He sucked it up and tried to act cool.

'I suppose you think you're funny,' he stated.

I shook my head, oozing confusion.

'Well, I've got news for you, mate. You're not. *I* don't think so. *They* certainly don't think so,' he seethed, pointing at the door, 'and the only thing you're going to achieve with this kind of attitude is a one-way ticket out of this school. Do I make myself clear?'

No. You're a twat. How do you 'achieve' a ticket, you idiot?

How was I supposed to reply to this question? If I pussied out and said 'sorry', like he wanted to hear, then I'd be admitting guilt. But that was the point! Guilt of what? He hadn't made himself clear, and I didn't know what the hell it was I had supposedly done so wrong!

I bit the bullet.

'What did I do?' I asked as sincerely and timidly as possible, so as not to aggravate his alpha-male complex.

He stared at me for a long time and, once again, I waited for him to explode. And, once again, he didn't.

'What's your name?' he squinty-snarled.

The quivering rebel inside me was pressing for a pseudonym – 'Yuri D Kedd'? – but the quivering tit inside me told him the fake truth.

'Jack.'

I chose not to mention my surname, as it sounds kind of made up, and I didn't want to push the twat over the edge.

'Come with me, Jack,' he said, grasping my elbow and herding me back into the common room.

'Right!' he called to the freshly silenced roomful of people. 'This ... time-wasting idiot ... '

Did that twat just call me an idiot?

A large vat of anger began to boil inside me.

What the hell is his problem?

I was really beginning to hate him, more than I have ever hated anyone before in my life. And that hatred began to manifest itself in my cheeks with a ninja-like pinkness; and in my kneecaps, with a genuinely dangerous jelly-wobble. If that twat didn't watch himself, he was going to find himself face to face with the mild quiver of my bottom lip!

' ... claims he doesn't know what he did wrong!' the twat continued, receiving a confirmatory chuckle from my classmates. 'Can any of you refresh his memory and tell him what I specifically told you about books?'

'Notebooks out,' a handful of people murbled quietly.

Yes? And ...?What's his point?

'Oh!' he said, in mock surprise. 'Is there anyone here who didn't hear me say that?'

Everyone shook their heads. A couple of people actually said the word 'no'.

'So why is it that this clown is the only one who *didn't* hear me?' he said, glaring angrily.

The twat! He's so wrong!

'You said, "Notebooks out"!' I confirmed, raising my notebook in front of him (and secretly double-checking that it *was* my notebook and not a film magazine, or the zombie book I was reading, or my sketch pad, which is covered in doodles of nobs and boobs).

It definitely *was* my notebook. There definitely wasn't a nob drawn on it. I didn't see what the problem was.

'Come on, Jack,' he squinty-sneered at me again, tilting his head to one side and shaking it slightly. 'You're wasting everyone's time. I said, "No books out." You heard me. Everyone here heard me ...'

No books out? NO books out? Is that what he said? Is that what everyone else just said! I ...

It was a bit embarrassing but, come on! It was clearly an honest mistake! The class was tittering quietly at the silliness of the situation and the atmosphere in the room lightened ever so slightly. A tiny bit of weight lifted from my shoulders.

'I thought you said, "Notebooks out",' I explained quietly.

'Do you think I was born yesterday, Jack?' he asked, still surveying me with curious hatred.

Does he not believe me? No books/notebooks. What's not to understand?

The uplifted mood of the class took hold of me and I decided to play my trump card. It's a trick I learned as a child – if you're in trouble, but you suspect that your mum isn't 100 per cent furious, you can usually wrangle your way out of a total bollocking by doing something to make them laugh.

Did I think he was born yesterday? Unfortunately, before I was even three words into my response, I knew I had made the wrong move.

'I hope not ... ' I grimaced.

This was the point where I knew I should have stopped. But, for some reason, my lips carried on spewing words out.

Jack's brain to Jack's mouth – stop now! I repeat, stop now! Do not advance! Whatever you do, do not follow that up with ...

'Your poor mum ... sore vagina!'

Once again I expected him to explode ...

He did.

IN MY FACE II

It turns out that the whole twat-at-first-sight thing can work both ways, because Peter 'The Twat' Farleigh certainly made his mind up very early on in our relationship to hate everything about me. He had done that stupid thing that all egomaniac new teachers try to do: identify the enemy general (the naughtiest kid in the class), make an example of him, and take him down. He had WRONGLY decided that I was the bad kid, and he was determined to make an example of me.

So, he marched me out of the common room, down the stairs and out into the playground in plain view of every window, in every classroom, of the entire school. And then he exploded in my face.

He towered over me. Steam came out of his ears. Smoke billowed from under his collar. Then his face *literally* exploded in front of mine. (OK, not literally.) He roared, he boomed, he spat when he shouted, but I didn't hear any of his twatty words, because all I could think was ...

I think I have found our villain.

And that's when he *really* bollocked me. Not because of

what I had thought (how could he have known what I was thinking?) but because of the smile it had inadvertently tweaked across my lips.

For the first time in my life, and with only *months* before I finish at this school for ever, I got sent to the principal's office.

THE PRINCIPAL OF
THE MATTER

I sat there all by myself in the deserted entrance hall, on
Death Row (that's what we call the two chairs outside the
principal's office, where the bad boys get sent to receive
their punishment – a place I never thought I'd ever find
myself), which is located to the left of the front doors, just
before the entrance hall merges into the canteen. (A layout
that, only now, after writing it down, strikes me as a bit
strange. How many other buildings in the world welcome
you with an odorous greeting of grease and cabbage? Not
including James's grandparents' house.)

I tried to rub the feeling back into my arm where the twat
had gripped me the entire walk to the principal's office: he'd
squeezed my elbow so hard that I could feel nothing but
pins and needles in my little finger and the finger next to it,
which probably has a proper name other than 'sacrifice
finger'. (I call it 'sacrifice finger' because if I have to do
something gross, like pick my nose, or my ear, or my bum,
I try to use this one, because it is the finger least likely to
enter my mouth or my food. If ever that time comes in life

that everyone has prepared themselves for, that moment when, 'If you had to have one part of your body chopped off, what would it be?' actually happens, I would sacrifice my sacrifice finger.)

Le Twat had knocked on the principal's door and then stared at me with hate-filled dead eyes (you may have noticed that I just changed Peter's name to Le Twat: it makes me smile and it suits him perfectly, like a sleazy, French, comic-book villain – *'Ellerrr, eh em Le Twat!'* Do you think there are any people in France with that actual surname? I am so going to find that out. Although they would probably spell it 'Letroit'. Pierre Letroit and the principal, Monsieur Coquefaece). He hadn't waited for the principal to answer. He had simply turned and left, leaving me to deal with Monsieur Coquefaece all on my own when, eventually, he would poke his evil little face around the door and drag me into Nazi HQ.

My notebook was still clutched in my fingers. I waited nervously. It would only be a matter of minutes before I would surely come face to face with a suspension. My stomach began to churn.

'You might be waiting a while,' a bodiless voice called from somewhere inside the canteen, directly opposite me.

The bright sky was reflecting off of the canteen windows, which divided the canteen from the entrance hall, making it impossible to see who was on the other side, but my super-senses told me that it was almost definitely a female.

'You talking to me?' I asked, squinting into the brightness.

'Jack, it's me, you tit. Of course I'm talking to you! Do you see anyone else around?'

Oh.

It was '*her*'.

'Come here,' she instructed.

I didn't fancy getting into even more trouble with the Monsieur Coquefaece by vacating my seat on Death Row, but I was under orders from a girl, and that pretty much supersedes about everything else in the world.

Pretending to not be quite so eager or obedient, I fake-reluctantly dragged myself to the open doorway of the canteen, and there she was, just a dozen or so feet away from me, all by herself – Em.

(I hate that I still find her so frickin' pretty.)

'What?' I groaned.

'Can you help me?' She asked, wincing in pain.

'What have you done?' I asked, inspecting the situation.

The cheap plastic chair she was sitting in had a split down the back, where her long hair had managed to catch itself.

Now was my chance to be the hero. Here was a damsel in distress, and I was the only knight in sight.

JACK SAMSONITE: THE MOVIE

INT. CANTEEN — DAY

Jack steps forwards. He fearlessly wrestles
the tangled clump of hair free from the evil
clutches of the Dark Lord Plastic Chair.

                    JACK
  You're free. Go. Run!

                    EM
  I'm not going anywhere without you.

She rises from her chair. She gazes longingly
into his eyes. Jack rises, too. Then ...

[Damn it! Why do I always feel so wrong making dirty
fantasies about Em? One of these days, I'm going to find a
way to disable that big sappy portion of my brain and we are
totally going to do more than just hug. It's going to be
disgusting.]

FREEZE FRAME.
Jack and Em are paused in time whilst doing
nothing very exciting at all.

Her bio gently scrolls across the screen,
accompanied by some bland elevator Muzak.

NAME: Emma Ball

AGE: 17

PROFESSION: Librarian, or something nice and gentle like that

STATUS: Just really nice and lovely

MOTTO: 'I'm so perfect for you it's wrong.'

COMPATIBILITY CHECK: [Scrolling text with accompanying VOICEOVER]

PROS

- She once showed an interest in me. This means she has the CAPACITY to like me. I know of no other girl in the world with this ability
- There isn't a doubt in my mind that she is perfect for me (other girls would be a trial-and-error process)
- James knows I like her, so would hopefully not let her fall for his stupid, irresistible perfectness.

CONS

- She has already expressed her non-interest in me (two years ago)
- I don't think I'm her type
- James knows she's not into me, so may allow himself to fall for her irresistible perfectness.
- She's hot; I'm not.

Meanwhile, back in reality ...

'Let me just ... ' I began, as I gallantly entered the fray to free her entangled hair.

'Ow, crap!' she gasped.

'Sorry! Just ...'

'Ow! Jack!'

'Sorry, sorry! I'm just trying to ...'

'Ow! Stop, stop, stop!!' She sucked air in through gritted teeth. 'Remind me never to have sex with you. You're about as gentle as a robotic elephant!'

Possibly the most hurtful thing I will hear all year. (Unless the elephant bit was a compliment.)

'Sorry,' I muttered whilst she painfully ripped herself free, leaving a surprising amount of hair behind.

What I *wanted* to say was, 'I think I might actually be OK at sex! I reckon that after about ten or twelve practice runs I could last up to two minutes!' But I knew it would be no use. She doesn't want me. She made that very clear when we were fifteen.

'Sorry, it's just ... Jesus!' she complained, noticing how much hair she had lost.

She stuffed her notebook into her bag and began to walk off. 'Come on,' she ordered, then, 'How come you're not in class?'

'Because our school is being taken over by French comic-book Nazis,' I informed her.

For some reason she looked confused.

'Pierre Letroit frickin' *dragged* me down to the principal's office!' I explained.

'What?' she asked, half-shocked, half-confused about there being a French Nazi named Letroit at our school.

'And it gets worse,' I added dramatically.

'Worse than your flies being undone?'

'Crap!'

I had a serious problem.

JACK SAMSONITE: THE MOVIE

EXT. SCHOOL — DAY

The No.1 Dude and his two sidekicks are
discussing business as they patrol the
perimeter of the educational facility.

                    VOICEOVER
                (Frogman Reeman)
    Jack had gotten away by the skin of his
    teeth. It was just sheer dumb luck that
    the Nazi general — Monsieur Coquefaece —
    was absent that day.
        In fact, he was due to be absent all
    week. That's what happens when you fall
    down the stairs and puncture a kidney with
    your own snapped arm-bone.

                    JAMES
    Is that even possible?! Just the bit where
    the bone ripped through his arm sounds
    made up to me. And what are the chances of
    it poking through his back and into a
    kidney?

                    JACK
    Exactly. It's so unbelievable it *has* to be
    true!

                              TIM

    So, what do kidneys even do? Are they the
    things that digest grass?

Jack and James ignore him.

                              JACK

    Plus, Em's mum says it's true, and she's a
    nurse!

                              TIM

    Or are they the things that soak up
    nicotine, like they show us in biology?

Jack and James continue to ignore him.

                              JAMES

    Just because she's a nurse, doesn't mean
    she never lies! It's not like she's a
    priest or something!

                              JACK

    Oh, right, like priests are the most
    honest people on the planet. They molest
    choirboys!

                              TIM

    Or do they make spunk?

Jack all of a sudden stops ignoring him.

JAMES

Relax. He's confusing kidneys with
testicles again.

TIM

Duhhh! Testicles don't *make* spunk! They
just store it, dumbass!

Jack and James return to ignoring him.

JACK

Anyway, this isn't getting us any closer
to solving the problem.

JAMES

What was the problem again?

JACK

Asking someone to be the hot girl in our
film!

TIM

What about her?

Tim points to the first person to pop into view.

JAMES

That's not a 'her' Tim, that's a 'him'
with long hair.

And? What's the problem? First you kiss
him, then you can punch him. Or he can
punch you. That's both problems solved,
right there!

OK, enough of this script thing for now. I'm confusing
myself about what bits of my life are supposed to be real,
and what bits are for the screenplay. No, I know, it's all supposed to be *real*, and that's the point and everything, but
there are bits, like when one of your friends refuses to shut
up about kidneys, that you probably need to start to imple-
ment a bit of editing. Otherwise you're going to have one
seriously lame film.

'Isn't it kind of obvious who we should ask?' James
frowned.

Yes.

It is.

I think.

Is it?

What did that even mean? Does he mean we should obviously ask the unbelievably hot new girl to play the hot girl in
our film, or does he mean we should ask Em, because she's
the only girl any of us are actually good friends with? Or ...
*is he calling Em hot? Does he like her? I don't think I like the
sound of this! Do I have competition???*

Woah, woah, woah! Em isn't interested in me. I know
this. She already told me, so why shouldn't my best friend
of all time be allowed to be with my other best friend? (I'm
talking about Em there, not Tim.)

Because it's messed up! That's why! Just the thought of it makes me sick! It would be like sleeping with another guy's poo! We used to be very close, we weren't meant to stay together, we parted ways – that doesn't mean anyone else should kiss it!

But it's fine. He was probably talking about the new hot girl, anyway.

Wait. Does he like her, too? Because he can't! I bagsied her! Or, OK, maybe Tim bagsied her first, but he doesn't really count. But James can't go around thinking every girl I like is hot! That's just rude! Especially as he's much better-looking than I am now! I wouldn't stand a chance! OK, so I don't really stand a chance anyway, but I've already had to suffer enough rejection. She is my rebound. I NEED her!

Of all the nemesises in my life to choose from, I was certain Letroit would be the man for our film, but now – there is a horrible chance it could end up being my best friend.

SEAN PALMER: ARSE-FARMER

(That's my secret little nickname I made up for him. Because I'm clever.)

Yeah, I know, as if I'm not struggling enough to limit the bad guys in this story! What can I say? Maybe I'm a twat-magnet ('twat' here meaning 'dickhead', not 'vagina', unfortunately). As dependably wankish as Letroit seems, there's no escaping the fact that he is nothing more than a new entry. He might actually just be a one-hit wonder.

Sean Palmer, on the other hand, is a non-mover at number one. He has been a permanent monkey on my back for months now. Except, he's not a monkey, he's a gigantic great vagina, and he's not on my back, he's in my face. ALL THE TIME (but, as far as metaphors go, I'm thinking I should probably stick with 'monkey on my back').

I'm not sure exactly what it is about him that I hate so much, especially as he's never actually set out to wrong me in any way. Maybe it's because he's one of the most self-assured people I've ever met, or maybe it's because he just breezed over, completely ignored me, put his arm around Em's neck and said, 'You alright, babes?' as if they've been friends for ever. Or maybe it's because he's the world's biggest penis-brained-penis-faced-penis-handed-penis-monger I've ever seen. Do I have to choose just one reason? I could go on ...

To be fair, he's not actually the BIGGEST wanker I've ever met, but I think he gets even further under my skin for this simple reason: nobody else realises that he's a complete twat. Everyone else *likes* him! In fact, when it comes to Sean, they don't just like him – they *love* him! Even James and Em! But not me (in case you hadn't figured that out already). I've just had an urge to cram his nostrils full with his own toenail clippings since the day he started at our school, last year.

Thankfully, I have at least one like-minded accomplice in my Campaign to Undermine all Nobs and Twats. She is also my back-up plan, my hot-girl option three, and my first ever sighting of see-through knickers. Allow me to explain (not the see-through knickers bit – that's a whole other story) ...

BAD FANBOY

Maybe it's me. Maybe my twat-radar is just overly sensitive.
Maybe I should give him a chance.

Just when I was about to give up on my hatred towards the Arse-Farmer, I found an unexpected confidant in Little Miss I-Apparently-Love-All-Boys-On-the-Face-Of-the-Planet-Except-For-Jack-Samsonite: Sally Kirk. (It's not like she's mean to me, but where everyone else seems to get kisses and cuddles and sex, I seem to be invisible.)

There had been seven of us lounging around on the common-room sofas: Sally, Carlos, Alex-the-girl, Alex-the-boy, Iain Vinleigh, Sean and me. As usual, Sean was leading the conversation. Well, I say 'conversation', but he was actually the only one talking. It was more like Sean's story time – a recital of chapter eight in his autobiography, *The Awesomeness of Me*. Everyone was absolutely enthralled by Sean's (clearly made-up) tale of how his dad had once let him drive his van in an empty car park and he'd accidentally driven it into a dwarf. Twat. (Sean, not the dwarf.) Alex-the girl and Alex-the-boy were both laughing in all the right places; even the usually reliable Carlos was chuckling (but I'll let him off because he doesn't speak English as good as what the rest of us do, and may have just been laughing out of politeness, the way foreign people do); while Iain Vinleigh was literally on the edge of his seat, hands clasped between his knees, throwing himself back and forth with huge, excitable, posh guffaws at the end of every sentence (even the ones that weren't supposed to be funny).

No one was more captivated by this story than Sean himself. So captivated, in fact, that he hadn't glanced at Sally's gaping cleavage once. Not once (whereas I, on the other hand, had looked three times, which was the only polite thing to do, since she had gone to so much trouble to squeeze them out there).

'It was, like, has anyone seen that Coen brothers film, *Bad Santa*?' Sean asked.

The what! What the hell is he ... Bad Santa? *A Coen brothers film? Who the hell does he think he's talking to!*

'Oh, that film is *so* funny,' gushed Alex-the-girl.

Who the hell *was* this hack? He had come swanning in there like he owned the place, then presumed to overthrow my throne of movie-fanboy-ness with his Sky Movies, Cineworld and Michael Bay tutelage from the glossy school of big-budget wank!

I know my films and I can tell you for a fact that the Coen brothers *did not* make *Bad Santa*, and I was about to make that known.

'That wasn't a Coen brothers film, was it?' I asked, speaking for the first time, pretending I wasn't actually 100 per cent certain of the answer, (I didn't want to be as big-headed towards him as he is to other people).

72

'Yeah, it was,' Sean corrected me, like a total penis-face, too arrogant to bother pretending not to be sure.

'I'm pretty sure it wasn't,' I rebutted.

'No, it was,' he said dismissively, whilst trying to continue with his story.

Frickin' frick! If only my stupid phone had had full internet access (instead of being limited to email and Facebook)! I so needed to get on IMDb and prove this penis-brain wrong in front of all his newfound followers!

I decided that if I couldn't prove him wrong with fact, then I would just have to do it with fake fact.

'Well,' I had continued, interrupting his arse-faced story yet again, 'I'm actually reading the Faber and Faber book of their complete works, and it's not mentioned once in that.'

'Oh, well, it's wrong – I'd get over it, mate,' he smirked condescendingly.

No, you big frickin' wank-brained, arse-headed, monkey-nob-ball frickin' penis-willy! You're the one that's wrong! Get over yourself!

'I'm pretty sure it's right,' I replied, with a bemused smile.

'Mate,' he said, looking me in the eyes for the first time, 'seriously, I've been making 8mm films in my back yard since I was nine years old. Trust me, I know my films.'

I wanted to strap his nob to his face using the elastic of his own underpants, and then punch him. With his own balls.

You know NOTHING, you arrogant little 'I'm right about everything' nob!

'Yeah, Jack, I'm pretty sure he's right,' Iain Vinleigh spoke up, in his stupid, posh, 'I'm a stupid posh arse-faced nob' voice.

73

You wouldn't know the Coens from the frickin' Co-Op, you dumb, posh tit! Keep your nose out!

'Here, look,' said Alex-the-boy, pressing a few buttons on his phone. 'I've got the IMDb page loading now.'

Ha! Now we'll see who the big, toss-faced, know-nothing wannabe, movie-buff-hack really is ...!

Crap.

Crap. Crap. Crap.

Crap. Crap. Crap. Crap. Crap.

Crap. Crap. Crap. Crap. Crap. Crap. Crap. CRAAAAAAAP!!!

Yes, it was me. I was the frickin' arsehole who always has to be right about everything and was proven wrong in front of everyone else. It didn't matter that the Coen brothers didn't actually *direct* the film, and were in fact just two producers out of about eight: their names were on the IMDb page and that was all that counted. I was the prick. I was the arsehole. I was the one with egg on his face (whatever that actually means), tail between his legs, know-nothing on his nob, who had to apologise and try with all his might to wake up from the world's stupidest nightmare.

Crap, crap, crap and really, really, really, very much crap!

When the bell rang for lunch thirty seconds later (we'd all had a study period and were the only ones in the common room), everyone got up and left for the canteen. I made a tiny attempt to get Carlos's attention (I said his name quietly), because I desperately needed some form of conversation with someone to try and block out the deafening drone of humiliation that was reverberating through my head.

Sally was moving slowly as she gathered her things, almost as if on purpose to avoid leaving with the others. She had caught my eye and given an exasperated eye roll.

'What?' I laughed uneasily, hopeful the eye roll was for what I thought it was.

'Ugh,' she sighed. 'Nothing.'

Holy crap. Sally Kirk just <u>spoke</u> to me!

OK, so I'd always thought of Sally as being a bit of a standard, suburban town girl who was nice but thick: pretty, but destined to look rough in another fifteen years: totally snoggable, but not the slightest bit interested in me. But the moment she began talking to me, and her big dark eyes connected with mine, and her crooked red-lipped smile beamed in my direction, I found myself utterly powerless. She had that something that I can't explain; that thing that makes me feel very hot, very nervous and very not very good of sentencing words my together into very sensical stuff. She was one of those girls who could have told me to go down to the shops and buy her some condoms so that she could have sex with lots of other guys that weren't me, and I would have done it in a flash, simply to try to please her for just one second.

She then looked at me with a slight smirk and shook her head.

'What?' I demanded, returning her smirk, which was code for, 'It's safe. I'm one of you!'

'Is it just me?' she asked, protecting herself with vagueness.

'No,' I said, going out on a limb. 'It's definitely not just you.'

I was fairly certain she was talking about the twattishness of Sean, but there was a part of me that wondered if she wasn't actually talking about the explosive chemistry between the two of us.

'Ugh, thank god!' she sighed, with a mixture of annoyance and relief, whilst slumping back down onto the sofa opposite me; then, double-checking I wasn't completely getting the wrong end of the stick: 'We are talking about the same thing, right?'

'I think so,' I assured her, but not entirely certain myself. 'You mean . . .' And then I mimicked Sean, lounging back in my seat, resting my right foot on my left knee, one arm on the arm rest whilst using the other arm to make large and impressive hand gestures in the air.

'Yes!' she giggled, conspiratorially. 'He's a wanker, right? Oh, I was *SO* hoping you were right about that film! If it makes you feel any better, I thought he was wrong, too.'

It was the first time Sally and I had ever uttered a word to each other in the three years that she'd been at our school. It was also the moment that I fell a little bit in love with her.

JACK SAMSONITE: THE MOVIE

INT. JACK'S BEDROOM — NIGHT

Jack 'The Kisser' Samsonite, bored of watching
the *Antiques Roadshow* marathon on the
Yesterday channel, kisses his parents
goodnight, then makes his way up to bed. Even
though it is only a Sunday evening and he is
about to go to sleep, he still manages to look
totally ripped and casually cool, which is
lucky because, as he opens his bedroom door,
Sally Kirk appears to have somehow broken into
his house and just so happens to be sprawled
across his bed in nothing but lacy black
underwear.

P.S. You could totally see her nipples.

FREEZE FRAME.

Her bio slams onto the screen.

  NAME: Sally 'Upskirt' Kirk
  REDEEMING FEATURES: Hot
  STATUS: Gagging for it
  QUOTE: 'I want to do it with Jack
  Samsonite because he's totally, insanely
  hot and he makes me want to be really,
  really naughty and stuff.'

COMPATIBILITY CHECK:[Scrolling text with accompanying VOICEOVER]

<u>PROS</u>

- She's super nice
- She seems to think I'm sweet
- We have a common bond in that we both hate Sean Palmer (which also means we will always have something to talk about together)
- I may be slightly delusional, but I've got this kind of vibe that maybe she might be slightly a little bit into me.

<u>CONS</u>

- I think James likes her
- She's not entirely my type — a bit too glossy [Damn it! I can't start adding more entries to my 'my type' checklist! I don't even have a type!]
- It's possible that I am mainly attracted to her because I think there is a 0.5 per cent chance that she could be attracted to me
- She's already lost her virginity. Many times (why do I always want to spell it 'vaginity'?). So will have multiple other guys to compare my super-crapness to
- She's hot; I'm not.

THURSDAY – 1st BREAK

'I still can't believe you said "retard".' James smiled whilst shaking his head, refusing to ever stop revelling in my humiliation as we strolled down the corridor towards the canteen.

'Oh, like you don't say it every second of your life?' I reminded him.

'Not to other people!' he added, making a good point (it's a private-time-only word).

'It's not my fault, though,' I protested. 'I haven't been sleeping much lately and my brain is doing strange things without my permission.'

'I recommend you get a LOT more sleep, then,' he cruelly advised.

'I can't! It's too hot! I spend all night tos—turning!' I explained.

'Use a fan then, tit-brain,' James suggested.

'Why did I never think of that before?' I asked, more to myself than to James.

'Because' – he began, whilst trying to dodge seas of Years 7 and 8 on their way out of the canteen – 'you're an idiot.'

'Woah!' hollered one of the little runts, grinding to a halt and throwing his hands in the air, before turning to James. 'Gay boy! What the hell was that?'

It was my good old friend, the Pygmy Warrior General.

James was understandably shocked by this midget's outburst.

'I wasn't talking to you,' James frowned.

The little twat stared him out for a few seconds before strolling up to meet James face to face (well, face to stomach), closely followed by his giggling army.

'You don't want to be talking to me like that, Charlie-boy,' he told James, with cold, mini menace.

Charlie-boy? What the hell is a Charlie-boy? Is this tit trying to create his own insults? That is so *two years ago.*

James sighed, smiled, turned his back, muttered 'Piss off, you little prick,' and we continued walking to the canteen.

Damn! That was actually quite cool! James was just cool! And he didn't even go red!

But, just then, the back of James's head was splatted with a handful of the Pygmy Warrior General's chips. (What kind of people eat chips at 10.30 a.m.? What kind of school *serves* chips with breakfast?)

'Watch your back, gay boy!' the little runt called, before turning to leave with his hysterical Munchkin followers.

James ground to a halt, brushed the back of his hair, turned, picked up one of the offending fried potatoes, then called out to his new Oompa-enemy.

'Yo, Bieber!'

The arrogant little nob spun round to unload as much

abuse as his little body could muster, but before he even got his first word out, James had made his counter-attack.

'Eat chip!' he called as he launched the oversized french fry through the air. And, just as I was thinking James had reached the coolest moment of his life, he achieved the impossible. It was the kind of chip-throwing super-coolness that the rest of us mortals merely dream of. As jaw-droppingly unbelievable as it may sound (I swear to god this is the absolute truth), the spinning ninja-chip zipped across the corridor and caught the little Pygmy right between the eyes!

Then, as cool as if this was just another day in the life of a chip-throwing legend, James turned and went on his way.

I *WISH* I could end the story here, so that we might all bathe in James's stand for the common man. But, as we all know, nasty little Pygmy Warriors do not take kindly to having their food hurled back into their faces. As James and I sauntered into the canteen, a hale of squishy potato bullets tore us to pieces. But we didn't care. We shifted into slo-mo, ignoring the plague of pricks that swarmed angrily around us as we revelled in the beauty of that chip-between-the-eyes retaliation.

I am JackMan and he is Chip Ninja!

I am Thelma and he is Louise!

I am Butch Cassidy and he is ...

He is the idiot who slipped on some ketchup and landed flat on his back in front of a canteen full of people.

I am Laurel and he is Hardy.

FINDING A VILLAIN:
BREAKING NEWS

Finding the perfect villain isn't turning out to be as easy as I'd expected. So far, we have three top contenders:

1. **Sean Palmer. He isn't much of a fight-starter though, just a standard wanker. And, even if he did fight, he'd have half a dozen followers tagging along, which, even for a superhero, seems a few too many (plus, we'd have too many villains).**
2. **Tyler the Pygmy Warrior General. He is my ideal opponent. He's a bully. He's tiny. He's a complete nob. Unfortunately, my superhero character might not look too heroic beating up an eleven-year-old kid.**
3. **Letroit. He is quite possibly the worst person to pit myself against. Yes, he is a twat, but he is also HUGE. Plus, making the perfect film by getting into a fight with the vice principal is a sure way of getting expelled, which may**

damage my chances of getting into a good uni somewhat.

The bit about Letroit being a bad choice of nemesis is actually a very good point, and one that I need to remedy as soon as possible ...

STILL 1st BREAK –
ELIMINATING LETROIT

Letroit was a fresh enemy: his hatred for me hadn't had time to solidify yet. It was just a misunderstanding. So, I took it upon myself to be the better man. I was going to explain, set the record straight, wipe the slate clean and start anew with him. They say that enemies make the most interesting friends; plus, I could really do without having the vice principal out for my blood at this juncture of my life.

So, whilst James was in the toilets cleaning squashed chips from his butt I, too, went on a mission to rid myself of a large, bland and unwholesome vegetable ...

'Hello?' called Letroit's *troit*-ish (stop pronouncing it 'Troyt' – it's 'Twat') voice from the other side of his office door, in answer to my knock.

I nervously turned the handle and entered.

This is such a bad idea.

'Oh, right!' he said with a faint smile and raised eyebrows, in a *This should be good* kind of way. He settled back into his seat, eyeing me with interest as I shuffled into his office.

'Close the door, take a seat,' he instructed with restrained glee.

I didn't want to close the door *or* take a seat; I just wanted to quickly apologise (for something I hadn't even done) and make a swift exit. But Letroit obviously had other ideas. He wanted to hold me captive and watch me squirm, like a spider he'd caught under an upturned glass.

But I did as I was told. I closed the door; then sat at the less spacious end of his cramped little office.

'What can I do for you?' he asked, giving me his full attention, then quickly deciding that I didn't deserve it, so promptly powered up his laptop, then changed his mind again and opted to maximise my discomfort with a cold and unblinking glare.

'Umm ...'

Everything I'd rehearsed on my way there had completely left my head. I had wanted to apologise in a very under-handed way; a way that would do the official business of saying sorry, but without giving him the satisfaction of sounding desperate and grovelly. But, now that my brain had apparently failed me, I was just going to have to make something up and wish for the best.

'Sorry about saying about your mum's ...'

No. No. NO! A different approach. Quickly!

'I ... er ...'

His deep-set, heavy eyes did not look impressed.

'How did your meeting with the principal go?' he cut in.

'Erm ...'

What do I say?

I didn't want to tell him that the principal hadn't been in

(even though he'd probably find out sooner or later anyway), because Letroit would just find some alternative punishment for me, so I chose my response very carefully.

'Kind of ... uneventful.' I shrugged.

Letroit looked surprised, then strangely resolute (which, I assume, was because he remembered that he has the power to convince the principal to unload as much punishment on me as he likes).

'Well,' I began, grasping the opportunity to explain the innocence behind the situation. 'The whole thing was a bit of a misunderstanding and I ...'

'I didn't misunderstand anything, Mr ... what's your name again?'

'Sam ... sonite,' I told him, reluctantly.

'Well, believe it or not, Mr Samsonite, I am actually capable of knowing a troublemaker when I see one,' he smirked, troitishly.

Is he implying that I'm the troublemaker? How do I tell him he's stupidly, wankishly wrong without making him angry?

'I didn't mean to, though. I'm not normally a troublemaker,' I tried to explain. 'I just misheard what you said, so I ...'

'So you decided to be absolutely bloody VULGAR!' he shouted, turning unexpectedly purple, unexpectedly fast.

I was too shocked to speak straight off the bat. He had taken me by surprise. This was not going to plan at all.

'Yes?' he urged.

'Sorry,' I offered, like a meek little mouse with no penis, 'I was trying to be funny, but—'

86

'Oh, you were trying to be *funny*? No! Newsflash, my friend. That was not funny. That was nowhere *near* funny! That was downright DISGUSTING!' he raged, veins bulging, spit flying from his mouth. 'And if I catch you talking like that again, you will be out of this school so fast you won't know what's hit you. Do I make myself clear?'

'Yes,' the penisless mouse squeaked.

You're a twat.

'DISGUSTING!' he repeated, after a strangely long pause. Then, 'No! Apology not accepted ... because I don't believe you mean it. I think you're a devious little ... trying to make life easier for yourself. Well, newsflash – you've met your match with me, Sampson! I wasn't born yesterday! Do you understand? I see kids like you time and time again and you're all the same. Newsflash – a new day has dawned in this school, and disruptive behaviour like yours will not be tolerated! Do I make myself clear?'

'I—'

'Those are good kids up there,' he said, at normal volume now, pointing a thumb at the ceiling. 'Do you think they deserve to have someone like you disrupting lessons like that? Ruining their education? Well, you may not have any interest in bettering yourself, but those kids have a right to learn, and I will not allow you to get in the way of that! Have I made myself clear?'

Yes. You're a big frickin' twat.

'Apology not accepted, Sampson. Nice try, but no such luck. If you want me to believe you're not a troublemaker, you're going to have to change your ways and *prove* it. Because, so far, all I've seen from you is reason after reason to recommend you for expulsion from this school. Do I make myself clear?'

If he threatens to expel me, or says, 'Do I make myself clear,' or NEWS-frickin'-FLASH one more time, I am going to frickin' ... I don't know what, but it's going to be ... I'm going to ... find out where he lives, break into his house, wee in his mouthwash and shit on his pillow!

Enemies make the most interesting friends, my arse! Enemies make the best targets for pillow-pooing, mouthwash-weeing and pant-peppering. Now, that's *my* idea of revenge. And I might just frickin' well try it! Oh, yes, Letroit, I *will* piss in your Listerine!

2rd PERIOD: MEDIA STUDIES

Sometimes I think teachers see it as their job to not only teach us English, maths, science and wotnot, but to also teach us valuable life lessons that we will all come up against in the adult world. Things like: *bad behaviour always pays off in the end because the teacher will get suckered into the bad boy's sob story, take pity on him, then go way beyond the call of duty to help him out at the last minute, practically write his essays for him, and completely ignore all the kids who genuinely care about learning and actually want some teacher-guidance!* Or other life lessons like: w*orking hard is futile because, when you are given a ridiculously short deadline for a media studies project, someone will relentlessly make it as difficult as possible for you to reach that deadline.*

Of course not! Don't be silly, Jack. That doesn't make any sense!

I'm right, you know; that doesn't make any sense. So why the hell, when we have to have our films finished for Monday, is Ben Marshall insisting on giving us a Film History lesson, instead of letting us go and film our projects?

Every second counts! We need to choose who's playing the lead, find a girl for me to snog, come up with some sort of villain to fight, then film the thing, add the music, edit it . . . and we haven't even come up with a story yet! We're in such deep poo! We need to start filming something!

This sense of urgency only makes film history even more unbearable. It feels like a big waste of time on a *normal* day, but today, when we really need to be doing more important stuff, like finding girls to kiss, it feels like torture. Film history usually consists of Ben showing one of my favourite films to the class, then pausing little sections, playing them back, over and over again, asking stupid, inane questions like, '*Why does the vicar that marries Eric and Ariel have an erection?*' (Yeah, seriously, I'm not joking. He actually asked this stuff!) '*What does that mean? What is the film-maker trying to tell us? Is it a symbol of Ariel's impotence from losing her mermaid tail? Is it a statement about male domination? Sexism? Inequality? Ariel has sacrificed everything for a man – her voice, her tail, her identity, her family . . . her FAMILY, which just so happens to be run by a dictatorial father. Where's her mum in all of this? Is that the last insult? She finally hands her life over to this man, and the vicar doesn't even have the common decency to not have a big nob-on? Think about it. Nothing makes it into a film by accident. Everything has a meaning. Everything has a purpose. That two-second sequence would have taken DAYS to animate; they wouldn't have put an erection in there just for the hell of it. Homework. Next week. I want an essay on what that means. Why does the vicar have a stiffy?*'

(My resulting essay, unlike some of my other essays, was

short, to the point, and 100 per cent accurate. It went something like this …)

In The Little Mermaid, Why Does The Vicar
Have Nob-ache at the Wedding?

He doesn't. IT'S. HIS. KNEE!

Even though I was the only person in the class to actually
give an answer that wasn't a rambling concoction of bum-
chutney, and was actually the *correct answer,* I also
happened to be the only person in the class to get an F.

Ben Marshall can chew my gruff-nuggets.

Anyway, today Ben has chosen to ruin *Batman.* All I want
to do is work on our film. Since, thanks to that 'F', I no
longer have any respect for him in the slightest, I have no
problem whatsoever in getting my notebook out beneath the
desk, sticking my mirrored sunglasses on so he can't see that
I'm not watching the screen, and getting to work writing a
plot outline for our film. When I eventually closed my notebook, I realised that the Batman we were watching wasn't
actually any of the new films; it was one from the 1960s that
I never even knew existed. I sat there, utterly bemused by
the weirdness of this film, watching a very camp Batman
dangling from a helicopter with a shark chewing on his leg.
Then I found myself slipping into Ben's over-analytical
mindset and wondering: 'Why *did* Batman keep a can of
Shark Repellent Bat-spray in his helicopter?' What did that
mean? He only had three different cans of Bat-spray in that
helicopter. How could he have possibly predicted that he

might get attacked by a shark whilst he was *flying*? If he hadn't chosen that particular spray he would have died! Or at least lost a leg. His whole life could have been changed by that one decision. He wouldn't have been around to stop the bad guys. Hundreds of people would have suffered as a consequence. The entire world could have been thrown into turmoil. And it all hung on that one decision.

Batman made the right decision. He is a superhero; they tend to do that. I am not a superhero. What if I make the wrong decision? What if I make *all* the wrong decisions? What if I mess up my entire life by making a series of dodgy choices? The right decisions are what separate Batman from Buttboy (the weirdo who leaves messages in the Griffith's Park toilets, like '*Meet in this cubicle, every Friday, 10 p.m. I'll suck you off for £20*'). There are so many decisions to make and I haven't got a frickin' clue what I'm doing!

Luckily, the next chapter in my life pretty much wrote itself.

LUNCH BREAK: TAKING THINGS TO THE NEXT LEVEL

It seemed like such an easy question to answer. The way it was asked, in that laidback, throwaway kind of way, made it seem like I should have been able to just spew up an instantaneous answer with just as little effort. But I couldn't. It was one of the scariest questions I have ever had to answer.

I knew I should say yes. Everyone else would say yes. 'Yes' is generally the normal response. Most people wouldn't even give it a second thought. It'd be like this: Question? – YES! In fact, there wouldn't be the gap for the dash thing. It'd be more like: Question? YES! Wait. Even that isn't right ... Question?YES! That's a bit more ... no, still, no. Maybe: QuesYES!tion?

Except I'm not everybody else. I'm freaky little me. So, when the question was all of a sudden sprung on me, I was kind of stuck for an answer. It went something like this:

Question? .... Ummmmmmmmmmmmmmm mm .....

I know what you're thinking – I'm a dick. I know! But, to be perfectly honest, the whole thing just scares the crap out of me. So much pressure to look cool, act cool, be an entertaining participant in conversations, not be a nob . . . I'll probably just spend the entire time feeling uncomfortable and paranoid! Plus (this is going to sound super-wet), I'd rather just stick to our usual routine of Trivial Pursuit, talking about girls, watching a movie, sleep over. That was actually the answer I wanted to give. But I didn't. You will be glad to hear that the answer I gave was 'yes'. Not because I actually wanted to, but because . . .

1. **Em was doing the asking, and she is kind of difficult to say 'no' to (she has boobs and stuff) and, in case you haven't noticed, I have this soft spot for her**
2. **James had already jumped at the chance to say 'Yes!' which meant, even if I did stick to the usual Friday night routine, it might be kind of odd if I went round to his house, played games, watched a film and talked about girls with his mum and dad.**

But, much to my own surprise, my answer was 'Er . . . I dunno.'

That's right, I was sitting on a common-room sofa, sandwiched between two awesomely hot girls, one of them asked if I wanted to go to the pub (as part of a big group, not as a date or anything), and I didn't jump at the chance!

'Oh, come on!' Em yelled, sounding exasperated, rather than pleading. 'You never come out!'

'You never go out?' Edith queried, reprimandingly.

Great. Another reason for her to hate me.

'I live in the middle of nowhere,' I explained (didn't bother mentioning the bit about 'going out scares me').

'It's always more fun when Jack comes out,' Em informed her.

Is she being serious or is she taking the piss?

'Are you taking the piss?' I asked.

'No, I'm not taking the piss!' She laughed. 'I was paying you a compliment, Mr Paranoid!'

'Oh,' I smiled smugly, 'really?'

Jesus, it must be SUPER dull when I'm not there, then!

'Well,' Em rectified, 'it's not like you're the life and soul of the party, but *I* have more fun when you're out.'

Holy crap, I don't think she could really make this much clearer ... I think she does like me!

'Go onnnn, come out!' Edith urged.

I'm not usually the type to buckle under peer pressure, but there was no way I was going to miss out on this.

'Hmmmmm ...' I pondered, pretending to still be unconvinced.

Of course I was going to go. They were practically *begging* me to go!

This is brilliant! I'd pay money to go out now! I can't wait!

'You'd get to meet *Chaaaarlieeeee*!' Edith added, with a sly grin and a knowing wiggle of her eyebrows at Em.

Who the hell is Charlie?

'Who's Charlie?' I asked, doing my best impression of casual.

'No one,' Em said quickly, and shot Edith a warning glare.

*I DON'T WANT TO MEET CHARLIE! I **HATE** CHARLIE!!! Stupid frickin' Charlie.*

'I'm not even sure if I can go,' my mouth said, without even consulting my brain.

'What?' Em protested.

'My mum's working evenings, so I might not be able to get a lift home,' I explied*. (My mum hasn't worked evenings since I was about eight.)

'Stay over if you want,' Edith shrugged, as though it was the smallest big deal in the history of the world.

Stay . . . ? She . . . ? I . . . ?

Edith? EDITH???!!!! I thought she hated me! Her brother. LIC. Me. Retard . . . and now she's inviting me to sleep over at her house? What is going on here? Whatever *was* going on, it sounded very, very extremely very amazing, and I wasn't going to question it.

'Sleep over?' I questioned (OK, so I did question it a little bit). 'At yours?' I questioned some more.

'No', she idierred (like, '*Derr! You idiot!*'), 'at my grandma's! What do you think?'

She wants me to sleep over?

She wants *ME* to *SLEEP OVER!*

Me and Edith, alone, with sleep!

---

* 'Explied' is my new word, combining 'explained' and 'lied' into one.

My brain could not quite make any sense of this. Is it a trap? Is it a trick? Is it a joke? Is it going to end with lots of people laughing at me? It seemed a little too good to be true.

And what is she doing now? Why is she looking at me like that?

She was peering at me like I was weird. And . . .

I think she's waiting for some kind of reply!

My brain quickly weighed up the situation: *Hot girl – doesn't like me – invites me to sleep over . . . sleep over . . . hot girl. Say yes!*

'Yes!'

Now try it again, only less weird and freaky!

'That'd be cool . . . thanks,' I replied casually, mimicking her laidback-ness. Yeah, that's right, I'm cool. I'm all chillin' and down with the girly sleepovers and stuff (except inside I was doing a little dance and singing a clappy-hands song: '*Nob-ache, nob-ache, I've got nob-ache, tra-la-la and a girl's va-gi-na!*').

And now it begins.

And now my virginity has a graduation date.

And now I'm super-confused.

And I'm also crapping myself. But I know it's what I need to do. 'Out' is where things happen. 'Out' is where stories develop. 'Out' is where girls and guys get it on. And that's what's going to happen. I am going to get it on. And we are going to get it on camera (or, at least, a teensy bit of it). And I will be a superhero, star of a film, who kisses girls. My life will finally be transformed. I will finally be cool . . .

As long as nothing goes wrong.

First things first, I had to improve my chances of success and convince Edith that I'm not a total arsehole when it comes to mental illnesses.

AN EXPLANATION
IS FUNDAMENTAL

A perfect romance had been handed to me on a plate, which could seriously improve my screenplay, our superhero film, my life ... Edith, for some reason or another, had invited me to 'sleep over' at hers.

I must not mess this up.

I had to make sure the road ahead was free of all obstacles and obstructions. I had to repave my image. I had to reassure Edith that I'm not the shallow, narrow-minded idiot that my 'retard' slip had portrayed me to be.

'So, Em,' I said, casually changing the subject in a not-at-all-obvious way, 'I was just wondering if you wanted to sponsor me for Red Nose Day?'

Oh, I'm a frickin' genius!

'Errr ... I suppose. What you doing?'

Crap. Should probably have thought this through!

'Sponsored swim, to raise money for ... '

Crap, bollocks, piss! Think of a disability! Nothing that's too obvious.

' … ass-burgers,' I finally managed, without too much of a pause.

Phew!

'Are you taking the piss?' Em replied.

Erm …

'No.'

'You know all the money you raise for Red Nose Day goes to Comic Relief? You can't give it to a different charity!' Em informed me.

Not quite so genius.

'And … ' began Edith, taking the baton.

This isn't going to be good.

'It's pronounced As-pair-jers, not *assburgers.*'

Very not genius!

'No, I know,' I smiled reassuringly. 'Sorry, I should have explained … '

I REAAAALLLLY hope this works …

'My cousin has As-pair-jers, but when he was little he pronounced it ass-burgers, and that became his nickname, just as a joke. He doesn't mind! He likes it!' I was quick to mention. 'And I'm doing a sponsored swim *for him*, because he can't swim, because he's too as-pair-jery, and he's giving the money to Comic Relief. You see? I'm doing a … '

'You should probably explain it that way in future,' Em advised, with big fake understanding nods.

I'm not entirely sure she believes me.

'Sorry,' I laughed bashfully. 'I'm a bit of a retard.'

*CRAAAAAAAAAAAAAAAAAAAAAAAAAAAAAAAAAAAAAA
AAAAAAAAAAAAAAAAAAAAAAAAAAAAAAAAAAAAAAAA
AAAAAAAAAAAAAAAAAAAAAAAAAAAAAAAAAAAAAAAA*

AAAAAAAAAAAAAAAAAAAAAAAAAAAAAAAAAAAA
AAAAAAAAAAAAAAAAAAAAAAAAAAAAAAAAAAAA
AAAAAAAAAAAAAAAAAAAAAAAAAAAAAAAAAAAA
AAAAAAAAAAAAAAAAAAAAAAAAAAAAAAAAAAAA
AAAAAAAAAAAAAAAAAAAAAAAAAAAAAAAAAAAA
AAAAAAAAAAAAAAAAAP!!!!!!!!!!!!!!!!!!!

FROM BAD TO WORSE

I half expected Edith to turn around and slap me in the face, get to her feet and say, 'I hate you, Jack Samsonite, and you're *never* sleeping over at my house!' then storm away in a fit of sobs. But, somehow, I managed to save myself by explying how my family uses the 're' word in an attempt to remove the stigma for my cousin's sake, the way black people have done with the 'N' word.

'We've taken the word away from the bad people and made it our own!' I explained.

The fact that she made no verbal indication that my invitation has been revoked leads me to believe that I am safe. I think. Though a proper apology is probably a good idea, just to make sure. I *will* fix it. It *will* be good!

However, unfortunately I cannot say the same about everything that has happened since then.

It is 7.42 a.m. Friday. Tonight I am sleeping over at a hot girl's place (I hope). I am on the bus on my way in to school. And something bad has happened. There was no major catastrophe, no huge embarrassment, no terrifying death threats. All that happened was these two things:

1. **I looked in the mirror**
2. **My dad had his shower ten minutes too late.**

The bad news is that these two minor events may well just ruin the rest of my life.

Let's start with that 'looking in the mirror' thing. I suppose the really bad thing about looking in the mirror was mostly due to what happened last night, rather than what happened this morning. But it was still the mirror's fault.

I'd been getting ready for bed and everyone else was already asleep, so I spent longer in the bathroom than a normal person would. This meant that I spent quite some time making sure I looked as perfect as possible for the upcoming evening out. The first thing I did, obviously, was to get naked and measure my willy, which meant nothing to me since I don't know what the average measurement is (though I'm pretty sure anything under two and a half inches isn't very impressive, so I decided I'd try again later). I also inspected my armpit hair (OK, that sounds weird, but I fear that I may be lagging behind in the armpit area of puberty – so far I only have a feeble gathering of baby hair stuff, which is kind of embarrassing at seventeen!) and had the most thorough bath I've ever had in my life. I don't think anyone has ever had cleaner boy-bits than I had right then. Ideally, I'd have liked to have showered first thing in the morning (maximum freshness for my special evening), but there's never enough time with everyone fighting for the bathroom. And, for some reason, I felt the need to make sure that my toes were really clean, too (I don't know how these girly sleepover things work!).

Unfortunately, despite my knowledge of what happens if you spend too long in front of a mirror, I was still unable to prevent the inevitable from happening.

Don't do it, I warned myself. *It only ever ends badly.*

But, unfortunately, my brain wasn't listening to my mind.

I'll just do a couple, my brain replied. *It will be a carefully controlled and monitored situation. As long as it's done in moderation it is perfectly safe. Nothing will get out of hand, I promise.*

And in the end my brain got the better of me. Sure enough, it all started out fine: my brain was good to his word and nothing got out of control. And that's when I let my guard down. The addiction began to take hold of me. My need for more was infecting my sense of reason. After three I wanted four, after four I wanted five, then six, then seven . . . no amount was ever enough! I was unstoppable. I needed more! More! MORE!

And then it was over. It wasn't until I drew blood that I began to see sense. It was like a warning light – red means stop! The magnitude of what I had done began to bear down on me like a ton of bricks. I stepped away from the mirror and assessed the damage.

Oh, crap.

A hot, sweaty panic suddenly hit me like a burning fever. *What did you do? WHAT did you do?!*

But what I had done wasn't relevant any more. I knew perfectly well what I had done. The question I needed to ask myself was, 'How are you going to fix this, you idiot?'

THE END RESULT

I stood there in a wash of horror, dumbstruck by my own stupidity. I had mauled every single blackhead, spot and blemish on my face and, as a result, looked like I had been attacked by a swarm of extremely stingy wasps.

I couldn't bear to look in the mirror a second longer. Every single glimpse of my face sent nauseating panic hurtling into my stomach. I gently tried to wash away the red swelling with cold water, carefully dabbed myself dry, then applied a crap-load of antiseptic lotion. My skin screamed in protest as the furious inferno raged across my face, turning my hot sweat icy cold. I couldn't bear to think about it any more. I forced myself into bed and prayed that a dose of cool air from the wide-open window, plus a night of on-my-back sleep, would remedy the problem by morning.

MORNING HAS BROKEN (OUT)

The first thing I did when I woke up was to try to work out if it really was Christmas or if that was just a dream. The second thing I did was burst into a tingling sweat when I remembered what I had done to my face the night before. The third thing I did was look in the mirror.

Things were not good. Things were bad. Things were very red and sickeningly spotty. There was no way I could go into school like this. And, to make matters even worse, it wasn't even Christmas!

I'll have to take the day off.

But there were two problems in taking the day off:

1. My mum would take one look at my face and see straight through any pretend illness I concocted
2. If I didn't go to school then I wouldn't be able to go to the pub with everyone, which would mean I wouldn't be able to sleep over at Edith's, which would mean no getting it on, which would mean no romance for my film (or my life), which would mean damaging my chances of getting

into whatever uni I may choose, which would mean no career in the movies, which would mean a life of sucking nobs in Griffith's Park toilets for £20 a go.

Shut in the bathroom once more, my mum's make-up bag was calling my name. Desperate for something to help cover up the hideousness that was my face, I delved inside and, to my surprise, there wasn't just *something* to help hide my spots – there was a multitude of somethings! Pale eye shadow! Foundation! Even something called *concealer*!

How long has this stuff been at my disposal? How many years have I been needlessly humiliating myself by going to school with bright red spots on my face when I could have just painted over them with this bag of magic?!

Just twenty minutes of careful application (in a special-effects-movie-make-up way, and not like a boy-wearing-his-mum's-cosmetics kind of way), it was done. Fixed. Normal. Perfect! I was all ready to wow Edith with my clear and special face.

That was problem No.1 fixed. Problem No.2 was going to prove a tad trickier.

PROBLEM NUMBER TWO

Problem number two is exactly what it sounds like. There was a problem. And it was number two.

Once the make-up was applied things carried on as normal: I washed my pits, got dressed, mutilated three Weetabix for breakfast, went for a poo ... OK, rewind ... had my three Weetabix for breakfast, went to the bathroom ...

But the door was locked. My dad was in the shower. It was poo o'clock and my dad was in the shower!

No! This can't be right! Why is my dad in the shower?

'DAD!!!'

I called him at the top of my voice, but it was no use. He was in splash-city. You could drive a freight train into the side of his head and he wouldn't hear it if he is in the shower. Only my mum's shrill shrieks are ever enough to penetrate these walls, and she had already left for work! (OK, I'm blaming my dad for having his shower late, but there's a slight possibility that he might have had his shower at the usual time if I hadn't spent twenty minutes locked in the bathroom, putting Mum's make-up on. But, whatever the reason, it had caused a serious problem. A very serious problem.)

My poo was ready but the bathroom was not. And that was how it remained right up until the moment that I had to leave to catch the school bus.

This could possibly be the worst thing to ever happen to me.

THE WORST THING?
SERIOUSLY?

Now, to anyone else this might seem like a very minor problem. But I am not anyone else. I am me. And me cannot poo in public toilets. In fact, me has not pooed in ANY toilet other than the one in his house and the ones in his various holiday accommodations. He hasn't even done one at his grandparents' house!

It's not the first time this has happened. I've had to hold it in all day at least five times before. But this isn't an all-day problem. This is an end-of-the-world problem. Because I'm not coming home tonight. I'm going straight to the pub! And I'm not coming home from the pub. I'm going straight to Edith's house!

This is going to be the hardest twenty-four hours of my life (and Jack Bauer thinks *he* has problems?).

P.S. There may also have been a third problem last night, which I may not have mentioned because:

1. **I wanted to keep my list of problems to 2, because it's really clever to do that**

2.   I am trying to block it from my memory.

Unfortunately, blocking it from my memory is not an option. It is a BIG problem. It needs to be fixed, and it looks a little bit like this email . . .

> To. _Emmaball@memail.com_
> *Em, this is going to sound weird, but it's really messing with my head, so, sorry in advance for this . . . I know you said you're not interested in me, but I can't stop being interested in you, and I just needed to be sure, before I try to move on, do you still feel the same way, or do you think we have a chance together? Jack x*

I <u>KNOW</u>!

WHAT.

HAVE.

I.

DONE???!!!

It really wasn't my fault, though! It was my stupid, middle-of-the-night insomnia brain! It seemed like a good idea at the time! How the hell am I going to fix this?

ON THE BUS

'But *he* always manages to hold it in,' argued Pumpkin, my little, orange-afro'd, Year 8, regular bus-journey companion, after I unwisely shared my poo problem with him.

'How do you know?' I asked.

'Because it's shown in real time and you never see him go for a wee or a poo for the entire twenty-four hours,' Pumpkin explained.

'That's a good point.'

He may be the youngest and weirdest of all my friends, but he is also the wisest (in a really odd way). I think of Pumpkin as being my strange, little, motor-mouthed, ginger, guru.

Are those girls smiling at _me_?

'And he doesn't eat or drink either.'

'Yeah ... ' I said, thinking it over. 'Jack Bauer *does* have it tough.'

'Or do you think he does like the lorry drivers do down our road and poos in a bag and tosses it out of the window and into the trees for some curious old lady to stumble across, hoping it might have a brand-new lipstick inside?'

'You're dribbling on yourself,' I informed him, but he didn't seem to care.

They are smiling at me!

'Hi, Jack,' said one of the two girls, who were sitting diagonally opposite, and who I had just caught checking me out, shooting me a number of surreptitious sideways glances.

'Hi,' I replied, half expecting her to tell me I had toothpaste on my chin or something.

How does she know my name?

'How do you know my name?' I asked her.

'We've been riding the same bus for, like, five years now!' she scoffed with a roll of the eyes.

I don't know your name!

'So why are you suddenly saying hi to me today?' I asked.

'Sorry for being polite!' she laughed, then turned her back.

'No, but, you know what I mean,' I persisted, leaning forward.

OK, she was two years below me and was only 38 per cent pretty (she was cute enough, but there was something strange about her, and I couldn't work out what it was), but that didn't stop me from feeling kind of chuffed by the attention. She didn't reply, but she shot me another sideways-glance smile, which was driving me a little bit crazy.

'And how come you keep smiling at me like that?' I demanded, still feeling paranoid.

'I dunno,' she shrugged, 'you've just got an interesting face.'

An interesting face? Should I be excited or insulted? I know she's younger, but she could be a contender!

113

'An interesting face?' I pressed.

'You're funny!' she sighed. 'You're a colourful character and you ... what were you two talking about, anyway?'

'Shit in a bag,' Pumpkin told her, sharply, 'until we were interrupted by a girl with a nose like a shark's head!'

That's what's odd about her!

'Pumpkin!' she warned with a scowl (luckily they seem to know each other already).

'Speaking of shit in a bag ... ' Pumpkin muttered.

The bus pulled over, the doors opened, and on stepped Tyler (a shit in a bag, and, not forgetting, also the general of the Pygmy Warriors), with all the confidence of a Year 13, the assuredness of a mafia boss and the nobbishness of a total nob.

'Doug-ayyy!' he hollered to the bus driver, hand out for a high five, which the bus driver ignored.

Knowing he had an audience, Tyler continued his badboy performance: exaggerated, bouncy, shoulder-swinging swagger down the aisle of the bus, head nodding, gum chewing, hand raised, pointing a finger towards his pack of fans at the back.

'Tylerrrrrr!' some skank girls called (including two girls in Year 11, who take it in turns to sit him on their laps, boosting him with even more needless arrogance).

The rest of us normal people awaited his routine abusiveness as he made his way past us, phone blaring out crap music. His usual abuse-ritual normally involves the gum that he always chews either getting spat into someone's face or squished into their hair. He only ever picks on losers or geeks, which pretty much covers everyone that isn't sitting at the back of the bus. He doesn't care how old or big his victims are, either.

Today we are lucky. Tyler has decided he wants to keep his gum in his mouth. However, his journey to the back of the bus was not without its casualties.

'Ginge!' he said, greeting Pumpkin with an opened high-five hand.

Knowing what was coming, Pumpkin did his best to dodge the attack, but Tyler's hand still managed to smack loudly into Pumpkin's forehead.

As horrible as it was to see Pumpkin bullied into a situation so belittling that he actually stopped talking, I have to admit that I was relieved to not be the victim of Tyler's power-game. Not because I'm scared of him (the little twat's only half my size), but because I know that I have too much idiotic pride to sit back and take it, which would mean Tyler's criminal associates in Years 10 and 11 would then be out to get me and, as much as I'd like to let this journal get more interesting, and as much as I need to find a villain for our film, I refuse to let that happen. I shall remain in control over whatever violence I inflict upon myself, and I am not getting hit in the head. I repeat: **I AM NOT GETTING HIT IN THE HEAD!**

'Hey, where's your gay friend?' Tyler called back, realising he'd forgotten to piss me off.

'Oh, he's off having gay sex somewhere, I think,' I politely informed him, before adding, 'with your dad.'

Tyler stopped in his tracks.

Bloody great. Now look what I've done!

What did I tell you about me and retaliation? I was certain

115

that Tyler was going to turn around and make his way back to me with a mouthful of threats, but he didn't have the guts. Instead he just stayed where he was, slowly turned around and shook his head.

'You're gonna wish you never said that.'

Here we frickin' go ...

THERE WE FRICKIN' WENT

Things rapidly evolved from bad to worse when Tyler shuffled to the back of the bus in floods of tears and I took a good guess that I'd definitely said the wrong thing. My fears were swiftly confirmed when the sympathetic voices at the back of the bus turned to angry ones and Tyler's two Gobby Skanks from Year 11 came to give me a mouthful.

'You just say summit about his dad, did ya?' the gobbiest one scowled as she and her friend came and invaded our space.

'Yeah,' I shrugged, pretending to be casual, but knowing that my red face was failing.

'You know his dad's dead, ya fuckin' twa'?'

'How would I know that?' I reasoned (which was obviously futile).

'So what you fuckin' talkin' shit 'bout his dad for, then?' she challenged, leaning across Pumpkin and shouting into my face.

'That ... doesn't make any sense,' I explained.

'You just go about talkin' shit about people's dads then, do ya? You fuckin' sunbed bastard? No! You're a fuckin' piece a shit and you should be fuckin' ashamed a yaself! How fuckin' old are ya?'

By this time she was shouting at the top of her voice.

'Seventeen,' I said, shrugging again.

'Seven-fuckin'-teen,' she sighed, shaking her head and looking around at the other people on the bus as if rallying the troops. 'You've got an eleven-year-old kid cryin' his fuckin' eyes out back there 'cos a you, you know that?'

I'd assumed that the question was rhetorical, but it seemed she was waiting for an answer.

'Well, maybe if he wasn't such an obnoxious little ...' I began.

'He's eleven fuckin' years old! He's a little kid 'avin a laugh! So he deserves a grown man mouthin' off about his diseased dad, does he?'

'Deceased,' her slightly less gobby friend corrected her.

'You what?' she asked, turning on her friend.

'You said "diseased".' The friend laughed nervously.

'What is it then?'

'Deceased.'

'Deceased, diseased, I don't know, do I?' she scowled, with a hint of a smile.

I smiled too, hoping to join in on the slightly lightened mood (something that, I should know by now, is always a mistake).

'What the fuck you laughin' at?!' she snapped aggressively. 'You ain't got no right to laugh! There's a little boy cryin' about his dad back there 'cos of you!'

She glared, inches from my face, awaiting a response, but I wasn't really sure what I was supposed to say.

'O ... K ... ?' I shrugged.

'No, it's not fuckin' OK! Don't you think you should at least be sorry?'

'Yes, I'm very sorry.' I sighed.

'Tell *him* that, not me!'

'I'm not telling him I'm sorry,' I told her straight up. 'He's a little tit and ...'

'He's a LITTLE KID!' she roared. '*You're* the fuckin' tit! You fuckin' Oompa Loompa twa'! You tellin' me you didn't like to 'ave a laugh when you was a kid?'

Oompa Loompa?! I'm almost six feet tall, you silly tart!

'I didn't used to spit gum in people's faces,' I informed her, crossing my arms in the hope that it would hide my trembling hands.

'Who said anything about spitting gum? That's not what I asked you! Answer the question!'

'Jesus,' I sighed, rolling my eyes as I realised this was not going to end.

And I was right. It didn't end. It went on and on like that for about another ten minutes, during which time even more of Tyler's friends had congregated around us to enjoy the show. Some (mostly the smaller ones) started throwing bits of food at me (what is it with them and food-throwing?) and spitting bits of paper, until finally the bus driver stopped the bus and ordered everyone to sit down.

'You're gonna get your face smashed in because of this, you do know that, don't ya?' Gobby Cow informed me before moving off.

The missiles and spitty paper continued to come, and Gobby Cow continued to return every couple of minutes to add something else she'd just thought of. She even came back down with her phone, whilst she was talking to someone on the other end (or maybe just pretending), just to try and intimidate me: 'Yeah . . . his dad,' she said, staring at me. 'He's a fuckin' prick . . . I know . . . will ya? OK, he's got a black T-shirt on and, like, creamy coloured trousers wiv all them pockets on and stuff, yeah . . . a big gay face and big gay hair. Yeah, smash 'is fuckin' face in, would ya.'

She disappeared to the back of the bus again, laughing, then a few minutes later came back to tell me: 'Just thought you'd like to know you're gonna get your face smashed in today. OK?'

'Oh. OK,' I replied, then, 'If they could make it to the Dog and Gun for about six thirty that would be perfect,' I added, but she was already on her way back to her seat.

'Just a little tip for the future,' Pumpkin offered, as the bus pulled up at school and we both got off. 'Next time you're struggling between two choices, like, wondering whether to insult someone or not, it's probably best to choose the *third* option instead. Do the *strange* thing.'

And, just as I was processing the weirdness of his advice, that's when Tyler launched his attack.

TYLER ATTACKS

I call it an 'attack', but really it was more of a spit-and-run. Tyler was undoubtedly aiming for me when he leapt from the bus and launched a mouthful of phlegm and chewing gum in my direction but, unfortunately for him, Pumpkin took the full force of the attack, directly in his face.

He screamed, he yelped, he writhed in discomfort, and ... you know when you get a bit of grit in your eye and it feels like it's the size of a pebble, but then it turns out to be absolutely microscopic? Well, I swear to god, I moved in closer towards Pumpkin to see how exactly a bit of spit could possibly cause so much pain, and, I kid you not, I watched an entire wad of chewing gum drop from his eyeball! The poor little guy was in agony! He was making strange guttural moans, stamping his feet, hobbling in circles, wiping his face on the shoulders of his coat (the arms had been sprayed when he held them up to deflect the shower of flob). He was making quite a scene.

I know this is *really* mean to say, and it makes me sound like a *total* arsehole, especially as the poor little fella had taken a hit for me, but ... if I'm being completely honest ...

as I put a comforting arm around him, I really hoped no one I knew was watching. I even looked around to see what kind of attention he had drawn. But, to my surprise, there was no one about. Just one solitary girl, standing all by herself, watched briefly from the entrance to the sixth-form block. Then, as she noticed me noticing her noticing us, she quickly turned and entered the building.

Edith.

What the hell was she going to make of *that*?

REGISTRATION

When I eventually got to school I could hear that the common room was already buzzing with a good number of people. I imagined that they were all chatting excitedly about going to the pub this evening. In need of some normal conversation, I was eager to get up there to join in with them. But there were a number of things playing on my mind:

1. That email I sent to Em. *PLEASE SAY SHE HASN'T READ IT!* (I need to rapidly concoct some kind of plan to fix this.)
2. CHARLIE! I completely forgot about Charlie! Who the frick is Charlie! If he *is* Em's new boyfriend, then that makes my email ten times more humiliating!
3. I am going to ask Edith if she will kiss me for a scene in our film tonight. That's right. I'm a movie star superhero now. I'm going to fix the whole 'retard' misunderstanding, apologise profusely, then I'm just going to ask her. Straight up. No faffing. Just watch me.

123

I didn't care about what had happened on the bus. It had left me feeling kind of weirded out, and I felt that maybe I should buy Pumpkin some kind of 'Sorry you got gum spat in your eye' gift, and perhaps explain to Edith that, even though I had my arm around a small ginger-haired boy, I'm not actually gay. But, right then, I had more pressing matters to consider, more positive things to focus on.

Trying not to show my battered and belittled confidence, I took large, carefree strides across the common room and tried to replay the smile from the cute girl on the bus to raise my spirits. It worked. She had said she liked my face! Yes! I had make-up on my face and it made me feel flawless. It also made me feel slightly fraudulent, in that Superman change-your-name-and-alter-your-appearance-in-order-to-trick-a-girl-into-thinking-your-someone-other-than-yourself kind of way. But it was a necessary evil. And it was only temporary. Besides, make-up is a lie that girls wear every day of their lives!

As I approached the busy corner where James, Em, Edith and Tim were lazing in armchairs. I was ready. I was going to come right out with it. Not weird, not creepy, not pervy. Just business. We needed a beautiful girl for our film, and Edith more than fulfilled that requirement. It won't be weird. We're all semi-adults after all. Plus ...

What the hell is going on here?!!!

My brain could barely comprehend what my eyes were telling it.

Edith is sitting on Tim's lap?

EDITH was sitting on TIM's lap!

TIM'S ...!

EDITH!

What is wrong with the world?!!

If anyone's lap deserves to get sat on around here it is certainly not Tim's (and is most probably mine). Why has this whole lap-sitting-on phenomenon completely passed me by? Why does everyone seem to get sat on apart from me?

I was obviously not the only person to find this scene a little strange because, as I glanced around, I noticed quite a few people checking this weirdness out. Someone who is easily the sexiest girl to go to our school for *years* was sitting on the lap of the freakiest little rodent to go to our school *ever*!

What's wrong with my lap? Apart from the bouts of unexpected nob-ache, what's wrong with my lap? Apart from the fact that I've got ... bollocks! I've still got dog crap up my leg!

Granted, it was dry, appeared to be odourless, and had mostly washed off, but still, the fact remained that after my super-duper extra clean bath last night, I'd gone and put on the exact same filthy dog-poo clothes from yesterday!

None of this matters. A girl on the bus was just hitting on you, and don't forget it.

It changed nothing. I was still going to ask her. Just as soon as she got off Tim's lap. Unless ...

Had Tim already asked her? Was this more than just a common common room lap-sitting? Is there something between them? Has Tim beaten me to it? Did he ...

'Heheh! What happened to you?' laughed James, watching me search for somewhere to sit.

Heheh! You know what happened to me, you nob! I got crap up my leg and forgot to put my trousers in the wash!

Then Em joined in, too.

'Oh, Jack! What the hell?' she chuckled.

Are they talking about my trousers or had they heard about the bus trauma? Even Edith's hand went to her mouth to hide a smirk! The only person not taking part in the laugh-at-Jack game was Tim, and that was only because he was so nervous about being sat on he was focusing all his concentration on where to look, where to place his hands, how to breathe in and out . . .

'Dude, go and wash that off right now,' James ordered, still laughing.

'It's clean!' I insisted. 'It's just a stain!'

'A stain?' asked Em. 'All over your face?'

Wha . . . ? Are . . . Oh.

THE BOY WHO WEARS
MAKE-UP

After pretending to be confused, then being assured by Em that I 'look ridiculous', I beat a hasty retreat to the men's room.

Holy Jesus, Mary and Mary's friend, Gethen, I am a twat!

It turned out that – outside the windowless, poorly lit, yellow bathroom at home – it appeared I had something on my face. In the bright daylight and halogen-lit men's room in the sixth-form block, I was suddenly made aware of what a huge amount of stupid I had slapped on my face.

I can't believe this is happening to me!

My forehead and nose were very clearly four shades more orange than the rest of my face, and there was a collection of very pale blotches splatted on top of what were very obviously large, raised spots. A long groan of nauseating humiliation rumbled from my throat as a few key phrases from the recent bus journey played back in my head: ' ... *you fuckin' sunbed bastard!*', ' ... *you fuckin' Oompa Loompa twa"* and, even worse than that: ' ... *you've got an interesting face ... you're a colourful character ...* '!

I want to be dead.

God, if you exist, please give me a sign; so that I may dedicate the rest of my life to you in order that I might one day make it into heaven and STAB YOU IN THE FACE WITH A BIRO!!!

BAAAAAALLLLLLSSSSSS!!!!!!!!!!!!!!!

1st PERIOD: THEATRE STUDIES

There is no word. I tried and tried to create one, but nothing quite fits. Not even all of the worst swearwords strung together are enough to explain what I am feeling right now. Words like 'humiliated' and 'mortified' are so inadequate that to use them for this situation would be like describing all the collective oceans in the world as 'a little bit puddly'.

If there had been a bus home any time before 4 p.m., then I would have jumped on it in a heartbeat. Sleepover or no sleepover. But there were no buses. Not until the end of school. So I stayed. I acted like a hero and stayed at school. Spots 'n' all.

I wasn't quite brave enough to go back up to the common room, so I've come straight to theatre studies class instead, and sat here by myself for nearly ten minutes, writing in my book, waiting for the others to turn up, to mock, to laugh, to see my spots.

'Where did you go?' asked James, when he finally turned up and sat in the seat next to me, at the back of the auditorium.

'Washed my face, didn't I,' I muttered.

Predicting the list of questions he was about to ask, I

began to wish that I'd spent the last ten minutes making up a good lie as to why I was wearing make-up, instead of just sitting there writing. But to my surprise ...

'Looks much better now,' he assured me.

No mocking, no laughing, no nothing. He was actually being understanding! He realised how embarrassed I was by the whole thing. He just let it go.

What's wrong with him? If the shoe were on the other foot (or spots on the other face), I'd be milking it for all it's worth!

And, to be honest, I think just a little bit of mocking might have made me feel less pathetic than I did right then.

I am so ridiculous that my friends have actually taken pity on me!

This was confirmed when Em came in, looked at me and said, 'Awwwww,' (as if I were a kitten) before sitting beside me.

'I had make-up on,' I admitted, sounding as pathetic as I felt.

'I know you did,' she smiled, her eyes full of pity.

And then she did something I had totally not expected.

'Awwww,' she said again. 'You're such a little Charlie-boy.'

And then ...

She HUGGED ME!

She's ended her no-hugs-for-Jack phase? After two years of an Em-hug-free existence, she chooses today to start getting physical with me again? What does this mean? YOU ARE MESSING UP MY BRAIN! What about Charlie? I thought he was your new ... What did she just call me? Did she just call me 'a little Charlie-boy'?

It's a phrase I've heard a few times around our school lately. I haven't got a clue what it's supposed to mean but, right then, I knew exactly what I *wanted* it to mean …

And that's when I decided that Charlie was gay.

Yes he is; he's gay.

(I knew it was very unlikely, but I was clutching to every strand of hope available.)

He could *be gay, though. And if there is a chance of that, then I need to resume my 'Get Em Back' mission straight away.*

So, obviously, I started with this.

'Your boobs have grown.'

Yes, I know. Smooth, right?

I can't believe I just said that!

She quickly released me from the hug.

Oh, dear.

'Ja-ack!' she gasped, covering her chest.

Oh, dear.

It was just an observation! She had squished them against me and I had noticed that they felt bouncier! I wasn't being a perv! It wasn't even a compliment! I've always been a fan of Em's smaller-than-average boobs! I don't care about size! Boobs are boobs!

'Well, it's true!' I defended.

'Oh my god, I can't believe you just said that,' she said, quickly busying herself with her books and pens and bag.

Thankfully she didn't look angry, she just looked embarrassed.

'What?' I shrugged, pretending not to be embarrassed, too. 'You told me I had a huge nob once!'

'That was different,' she insisted.

'What did he say?' asked James, having missed half of what had just happened due to messing around on his phone.

'Nothing,' Em said. 'Something rude.'

'What did you say?' James asked me.

'I don't think I should repeat it,' I told him, warningly (as if he hadn't already mentioned it to me at least a dozen times!)

'Did he say you've got big boobs?'

'No!' gasped Em, holding up a desperate *shush!* finger.

'It's true, though!' James enthused, excitedly. 'Last year they were like, meh,' (mimed little hills on his chest), 'but this year they're, like, WOOOO!' (mimed giant, bulbous mountains exploding from his torso).

Shut. UP! You are making this so much worse! Plus, I'm not sure anyone is allowed to talk about Em's boobs but me.

I quickly decided to take the focus off Em's boobs.

'So, what's with Tim and Edith?' I snooped. 'Is something going on?'

Em's expression suddenly turned from bashful to murderous.

'You fancy Edith?' she asked urgently.

'No!' I quickly blocked. *What the hell?!* 'I was just asking about her and Tim!' I clarified.

But before we could go any further . . .

'Circle, please!' called Connie – our large, ageing theatre studies teacher – with a few loud claps of her hands.

If I wasn't careful, I would end up making every possible-get-it-on girl think I'm a complete arsehole.

I really, really need to undo my arsehole-iness!

I was right, I really, really did, and since my arsehole-iness had focused itself mostly on Edith's LIC brother, I started with her. (I know, this sounds wrong, right? Suck up to Edith instead of Em? No. It's not wrong. It's right. Girls live in a world where jealousy rules their decisions. I can kill two birds with one stone here – I patch up the 'retard' thing with Edith, which improves my chances with her, which then makes Em feel jealous, which reignites her interest in me, and ... clever plan, right?)

JackMan to the rescue!

DANCES WITH ~~WOLVES~~
OBNOXIOUS IDIOTS

Before I had the chance to bottle it, I walked straight over to Edith and created a place for myself in the circle, right next to her, then proceeded to wince in pain as my elbow knocked gently into hers. She looked kind of puzzled as to how it could possibly have hurt me so much, when she had been barely even aware of it.

'Look,' I explained, showing her the bruise around my elbow. 'That's what that big fat twat of a teacher did to me yesterday.'

She turned away without saying a thing.

OK, that didn't quite go to plan. Try harder.

I needed to do something to make myself endearing to her, something to make me stand out from the rest, something like . . . a nickname!

I'll give her a nickname! It'll create a special bond between us and she'll think I'm all sweet and stuff, and we'll have our own special thing. She might even give me a nickname in return!

'So, New Girl . . . ' I began.

Nice nickname!

'My name's Edith,' she told me, unimpressed.

'I know, but you're also new . . . and you're a girl. I'll call you Edith if you'd prefer.'

Nice recovery!

'That's generally what names are for – written and vocal labels of identification. We should probably just leave character descriptions to the Native Americans,' she said, without even glancing at me.

Is she being playful or is she being bitchy? I can't work it out! But . . . if she's being bitchy and she hates me, then why invite me to sleep over?

'I'd love to have a Native American name!' I enthused, deciding that the bitchy thing was just in my mind.

'Really?' she asked, eyebrows raised. 'OK, I'll be New Girl and you can be Obnoxious Idiot.'

I think she IS being bitchy! One minute she's begging me to sleep at her house, the next she's treating me like a shitty-shoed, make-up-faced, retard basher. I don't get it!

I forced a laugh, but it hurt (not the laugh, the 'Obnoxious Idiot' thing). It hurt quite a lot. It hurt so much that I couldn't actually bring myself to say anything else. The wind was gone from my sails and, all of a sudden, I was not in the mood for the usual arm-flapping, skipping, jumping, screeching, spinning and laughing that were customary for start-of-theatre-studies-lessons warm-ups. I was beginning to wish I'd never spoken to her, and I was definitely regretting standing next to her.

Man, she is mean. Mean and scary! I'm not sure I want to stay at her house tonight! Or have sex with her!

Yeah, see how she likes THAT!

What is with her? Is she schizzo? Is she pissed about the double retard comment, or is this something to do with what she saw with Pumpkin this morning? Does she think he's gay? Does she think *I'm* gay? And, if so, is she being mean because she's a gay-hating Nazi, or because she's hurt that she can't have me?! I'm confused!

'Is this because you think my friend's gay?' I asked, somewhat out of the blue. Edith gave me the most baffled, shocked and . . . what was this other look she gave me? Was it . . . *scared*?!

'Right, right, right!' called Connie, clapping her hands with each word, quieting the class. 'Hey, hey, hey, hey, HEY!' she added needlessly, since we were already listening.

Drama queen!

'We have a new face, I see!' Connie smiled, 'Welcome!'

There was a gentle murmur from the class, unsure of whether they were supposed to respond to this. One person even began to clap, just one single embarrassing clap. (I so wish it hadn't been me.)

'So . . .' Connie left a dramatic pause, as if we would all be desperate to know what she had to say next, when actually no one gives a shit. 'As a nice introduction for the new member of our group, we will start the lesson with . . .'

Oh my golly gosh, the tension is killing me; could it by any chance be an 'Ice Breaker'?

' . . . an Ice Breaker!' she cheered.

Whoop-di-frickin'-doo. What an amazing surprise.

Then, as if to spite my prediction, Connie went and did

136

something I *hadn't* expected. Some kind of team activity would be Connie's usual routine for new faces (a game of trust, where you fall backwards off a table and everyone has to catch you is her reliable favourite). So I was more than a little surprised to see what Connie actually pulled from her box of tricks.

Balls.

Balls? BALLS! Seriously?!

I know she's not the greatest teacher in the world but, really, I expected more from Connie Decker! Or was this some new legislation brought in by the new Nazi vice principal, that every lesson must start with the throwing of balls and stating of names?

To her credit, at least Connie had mixed things up a bit: she had not brought just one ball, oh, no; this was going to be truly wild as she'd brought TWO! I know people always told me things got a bit more wild once you reached the sixth form, but I hadn't prepared myself for this level of off-the-scale anarchy! *Two* balls! Double the fun!

I am so not in the mood for this, especially after yesterday's incident with Letroit.

Connie explained the rules of the 'game' (game? Really? I always thought games were supposed to have some kind of element of fun to them), and the ball began its journey. First off was James, who Connie caught off guard, causing him to temporarily forget his name.

OK, as long as you remember your name, don't get thrown out of class and don't mention the teacher's mother's vagina, then this might not be so bad.

James was clearly aware that every second he kept hold of

that ball he was to be under the watchful eye of the entire class, so before he'd even finished 'telling us a little bit about himself' (we were all interested to discover that he 'Ermmm ...' and sometimes he 'kinda like ... I dunno, err ...' and also he frequently likes to 'ummmm ...'), he had launched that ball across the room. Straight towards me.

You twat.

In fact, he was a double twat, because not only had he chosen me to be the next victim of the hell ball, but he also throws like a girl. Desperate not to miss it and have to chase it across the room like some uncoordinated tit, I quickly reached across for his fast-moving curve ball, and that's when the (all-new) worst moment of my life happened.

FEELING. BAD.

James's entire body went limp and he could barely breathe as he tried to recite the incident to Tim, during first break. Tim was laughing just as hard, and he hadn't even heard the story yet.

'He ... he ... !'

But it was no use: every time James began to explain what happened, he dissolved into hyperventilated hysteria, holding onto Tim's shoulder to keep from falling down. If he kept this up he was going to pass out, and he'd deserve it, too.

'He ... oh god!'

And once again he was useless for another sixty seconds.

'Jesus,' I muttered, more than a little annoyed by the whole thing.

And then James reverted to trying to mime the actions of what happened, but even his arms were failing to function he was laughing so hard.

'What?' demanded Tim, buckling at the knees himself.

People were beginning to stare.

For Christ's sake!

I decided to get it over and done with and told the story myself.

'James threw the ball like a re ... girl, I went to catch it, and I accidentally grabbed Edith's tit. OK?'

No, it wasn't OK. Tim was almost crying with laughter now and I don't think James had managed to breathe in over two minutes.

'Inside ... !' James struggled to carry on. 'Insiderve ... !'

Bloody hell!

'And my hand accidentally went inside her vest top thing. Can we just leave it now, please!'

Of course they couldn't leave it. Or, at least, James couldn't. As soon as Tim realised that my hand had gone where he had only ever dreamed of going, and I had managed this without *ever* having to wear purple corduroys he all of a sudden stopped laughing. But, regardless of Tim's instant lack of interest, James continued to drag out my humiliation as long as he could.

But I am happy to report that, just minutes later, someone else's humiliation overshadowed my own.

SOMEONE ELSE'S HUMILIATION

When James and Tim had finally finished laughing at my boob-grab mishap, we began to make our way back towards our common room.

'Have you ever considered that your life might actually be cursed?' James asked, without a hint of a joke.

'Not *everything* goes wrong,' I said, defensively. 'If I'm lucky, I might get into a fight with some gobby cow's boyfriend tonight.'

'Seriously? You genius! How did you manage that?' beamed James.

But I couldn't answer because right then was when I encountered one of the greatest images to ever befall my eyes (not sure that makes sense, but it sounds good).

Julie Quill – my ex-maths teacher, and easily the hottest 'lady' in school – was restocking the tuck shop (which is run by the maths department and staffed by maths student volunteers, who are paid with sweets). In her arms were boxes of sugary goodness, stacked all the way up to her rack, and this overflowing bounty of beauty was causing her own bounty of beauty to overflow from her blousy of openy.

Candy and cleavage – I have never seen the two together, but now that I have, it's all I ever want to see again.

Being the normal person that I am, I took very fleeting glimpses of the awesome view, looking long enough to be able to memorise it, but not so long as to be noticeable to the naked eye (approximately 0.4 seconds). But Tim, not being a normal human being, was openly staring, and gawping, and making a kind of 'Ughhhh' noise. He was like a soldier stumbling across no-man's land in a fluorescent jacket and a neon sign strapped to his head reading, 'Idiot below. Fire at will'. He was destined to get caught, and guess what . . .

'Are you OK, Tim?' asked Julie, surveying his gormless face, her brow wrinkled quizzically.

'Ughh?' replied Tim, not even bothering to look up.

Step away from the pervert! Everybody! Disperse. Disperse!

The rest of us (being normal), allowed ourselves to gradually drift away from Tim as his and Julie's paths began to meet, like knights in a jousting contest, only instead of one of those long sticks they hold, Julie had sweets, and Tim had . . . Christ, I don't even want to go there.

'Are you feeling OK?' Julie asked, lowering her head in an attempt to make eye contact.

'Oh!' said Tim, finally snapping out of it.

And then he proceeded to say something that I will never forget.

'Sorry!' he chuckled, nervously. 'I was just staring at your goodies!'

The best part is, I wholeheartedly believe that, in all his innocent stupidity, he genuinely had not noticed anything but the sweets.

Unfortunately, despite my valiant attempts to disassociate myself from him, Julie had clocked me.

'Ja-ack!'

I'm not with him!

'Don't forget our interview,' she called.

Crap. I had completely forgotten – my careers interview. Julie has been assigned as my careers advisor and, in about twenty minutes, I'm supposed to tell her which university I've chosen! We're filling out the forms and everything! Which brings me back to ...

My Top 5 University Courses
(In no particular order)

5. **Broadcast Production at Poole University**
4. **Creative Writing at Newgwent University**
3. **Writing for the Media at Banbury University**
2. **Media Production at Michael David Institute for the Arts, Liverpool**
1. **Film and Video at Bowdon Media Institute**

Yeah, I have a list, which is all good and fine, but it's a kind of schizophrenic one. I don't want to pick a university before I've even decided whether I want to do film or writing. I want to make my mind up and choose one course or another: the last thing I want is to get accepted into a film school, then discover I actually want to do writing.

I'm supposed to have an answer for Julie in under half an hour. Christ, last Saturday it took me forty minutes to choose what DVD to watch; now I have half that time to make a decision that will affect/effect* (I seriously do not know the difference between those words) my entire future! What is wrong with the world? Why are we being forced to choose what we do for the rest of our lives when we are barely out of childhood? I'm going to be sixty-one years old one day, and I'll be hating the guts of seventeen-year-old me for making the wrong university choice and subjecting myself to forty-four years of sucking cock in Griffith's Park toilets! Talk about pressure!

Two years ago it was simple: all I wanted to do was make films and nothing could have *ever* made me change my mind. But that was two years ago. Today, thanks to the fact that I enjoy writing journals, there is a new person growing inside me, and he is betraying the old me.

My life is in freefall, spinning and plummeting at an alarming rate, and this morning I will have to choose where I am going to land. Sure, I can pick a spot and hope for the best, but when you actually steady your eyes and take a good look, the soft landings are few and far between.

I just hope I don't miss.

* Dictionary definitions:
Affect: to have an effect on.
Effect: a change which is a consequence of an action.
Braingoboom: a mild explosion of the head, usually as a result of trying to figure out the difference between affect and effect.

FIXING THE EMAIL PROBLEM

To reassure myself that there are things in my life that I *do* have control of, I have formulated a plan. I am going to fix that middle-of-the-night-insomnia-fuelled-love-letter-email to Em: I am going to hack into her email account and delete my message.

I can justify it like this: it's like a birthday present – until she opens it, it is MY email. I can do what I want with it. It's kind of wrong in the ethics and morals side of things (and probably the law side of things, too, now that I think about it), but it's a detour to the dark side that I'm willing to make.

Luckily I know from experience that Em only checks her emails every couple of days. I just hope that day isn't today.

Step 1. Try to guess her password.

Attempts I have tried so far:

1. Emball
2. emmaball

3. 22hillroad (At this point I expected her account to block me, in a 'three strikes and you're out' way, like mine does. Luckily it didn't.)
4. hillroad
5. about six different variations on her date of birth
6. Charliechaplin (her favourite actor)
7. Johnnydepp (her second favourite actor)
8. toystory (her favourite film. Or it was, four years ago)
9. jacksamsonite (I was clutching at straws and kind of dreaming).

It was around about this point that I gave up and clicked on 'Forgot Password?' The security questions popped up:

1. Your date of birth. (I know that one!)
2. Your mother's maiden name
3. The name of your first pet.

I didn't know the last two answers but, seriously? That's the extent of email security? You could extract that information from a perfect stranger in a five-minute conversation!

This could be very, very easy …

TROUSER MALFUNCTION #3

There are already two very big problems with these new trousers (#1. Dog crap up the leg #2. Continually dropping zipper), and I have now discovered another.

As James, Tim and I entered the sixth-form building, I broke away to go for a wee. The wee was great. I have no complaints: warm in appearance, mild in aroma (hints of popcorn and a soupçon of dandelion), full-bodied, bursting with spring meadow vibrance, and very, very refreshing. But it was post-wee that I noticed the problem. It was a problem that I had never experienced before in my life, because I had never owned pale khaki combats before. I have also, I realised, been living a life of blissful ignorance.

As I approached the sink and glimpsed myself in the mirror, a whole new world of toilet trouble revealed itself to me: the shake. It would appear that whenever you do the post-wee willy-shake, the drips do not all obediently fall directly into the urinal. No. Some of them drop all around your groinal regional zonal area.

Aside from being kind of gross and unhygienic, this has never been an issue with dark jeans because wetness doesn't really show up on thick, dark fabric. Unfortunately, on thin, pale cotton crap, it does show up. Very, *very* well.

There, in a four-inch radius from my nob-zone, was a pebble-dash-piss-splash effect.

Crappety crap!

Very quickly, before anyone else came in, I slammed the hand drier on, then rammed myself beneath it, keeping one eye on the door at all times.

Good news – thin, pale, cotton crap appears to dry fast under a hand drier. Bad news – I never realised how splashy the sink is.

Who the hell invented pale trousers?!

Bad news #2: My missed morning poo is really beginning to creep up on me.

Bad news #3: As soon as I began trying to dry the huge patches of sink-splash, the bathroom door opened, in walked Iain Vinleigh and the mission was aborted. Only half-dry, I panicked, exited the bathroom and ventured out into the big wide world. With wet pants.

WEE WILL ROCK YOU

Luckily, when I left the bathroom, there was no one around to see the watermarks around my balls. Now I just had to make sure things stayed that way until I dried up. I couldn't stay put, because it would only be a matter of time until people passed by.

Since it was warm outside, I figured that was the place to go. A short walk around the playing field should get the breeze on my nuts and I would be dry in a matter of minutes. Walking was a doubly good idea too, because it also seemed to help my poo problem. Every step I took seemed to help squish it back up, away from the exit and back into its little poo dungeon.

I stuffed my hands into my pockets and pushed them outwards, creating a sail-effect around my crotch, so as to catch as much breeze as possible.

I can't believe I've spent my whole life not realising that I've been splashing piss on myself six times a day! How did I not even notice this <u>yesterday</u>?

My world felt completely rocked by this piss revelation.

This is gross! Does it smell? Are other people able to smell this? Am I a stinky boy without even knowing it? I guess I'd better start putting all my lower-half clothing in the wash more than once a month. Stupid pale khaki combats! Why did I even buy them in the first place?

(The answer to that last question is this: I thought I was being clever. I thought that, since dark colours are supposed to have a slimming effect, then light colours would have the opposite effect. On my nob. I think I was mistaken.)

Then, as I made my way around the corner of the building, towards the playing field, I saw something that instantly took my mind off my fashion-fail ...

PEOPLE WILL STAIR

People! There were *people* outside! Lots of them! Maybe a dozen or more! *Silly me!* In my wee-wee-pants panic I had overlooked a very important fact – warm weather is not just for drying soggy balls, it is also for cooking lazy teenagers whilst they sprawl themselves across the stairs of the fire escape!

It was way too late for me to turn and run. They had all seen me. I was desperate to check the progress of the drying situation, but didn't dare draw attention to it by having a look. I bravely continued towards them, the *Jaws* theme beginning to play in my head, my paranoia beginning to kick in.

They're all talking about me. Looking at my balls. Laughing at me. Mocking me!

Loud voices and hearty laughs made it impossible for me to not imagine they were all having a laugh at my expense. And not just because of what had just happened on my balls, or the incident in theatre studies. It's a feeling I've had for some months now – an increasing paranoia that I am the butt of all jokes, the centre of all negative buzz. Every time I walk into a room I can't help but feel that at least a few people have just stopped talking about me all of a sudden. I'm sure it's not true. It's probably just a product of my neuroses combined with an overactive imagination but, today, something told me I wasn't just being paranoid. Just the look on Sean Palmer's face told me that a full-on Jack-slagging had just taken place. I could sense my muddied name still lingering in the air, like a bad smell. (OK, to be honest, it was either my keen senses and super-astute observations that alerted me to their recent conversation, or it was something I picked up on when Sean greeted me.)

'Speak of the devil!' he yelled. 'Here comes the nipple-twister now! All right, Jack!'

Nipple-twister. Great.

So they *had* heard about the theatre studies incident.

There was a small round of applause, accompanied by the *thwack!* of the imaginary potato that my brain had just hurled at Arse-Farmer's face. I tried to hide my emotional cocktail of rage, mortification and persecution (I don't think persecution is actually an emotion, but I don't know how else to say that I felt persecuted, other than the way that I just said it), then shook my head with embarrassed disbelief.

'Oh god,' I sighed with a smile, pretending to be a part of the joke, rather than the centre of it, then slapped my hand across my forehead. 'That was one of the most embarrassing things I've ever done.'

I was so desperate to be accepted by the group that I even made eye contact with Sean in a pitiful attempt at creating some kind of forced camaraderie between us.

'What happened?' asked Sally Kirk, with an understandingly sorry smile, eager to hear the details.

I breathed a deep sigh and attempted to perch on one of the steps of the fire escape.

'Woah, woah, woah!' laughed Sean Palmer, as he stuck his foot out to block my way. 'No sex offenders here, buddy!'

The unanimous decision that this was hilarious was enough to convince me to walk away.

You, Sean Palmer, WILL be my nemesis. My name is JackMan, and I will find you this evening, without your army of friends, and I will ... do something.

'Don't be a twat,' I heard Sally hiss in my defence.

I love you, Sally Kirk. You may have a reputation for being a bit of a slut, but I love you all the same.

Then: 'Oh!' gasped Alex-the-girl as she came rushing round the corner of the building, narrowly avoiding a head-on collision with me. 'There you are!'

Alex-the-girl has been looking for me?

'Julie Quill's looking for you,' she informed me.

Julie the Quill's been looking for me?

'What?'

'Careers interview? You're supposed to be up there now.'

I'm supposed to be up there now! I'm supposed to have chosen a university (or three)! I'm supposed to have finished my Personal Statement!

DECISION TIME

I dashed across the school and made my way towards the stairs that led up to Julie Quill's office. Not only was I in danger of messing up my university applications, but I was also missing out on the opportunity to sit in a room with Julie Quill, all by myself, for ten whole minutes! (They should really consider employing sexy teachers with huge boobs for every lesson – it'd really boost attendance rates.) I'm not sure Julie will be too pleased when I tell her I still haven't made my mind up.

Amy Norvich was on her way out of Julie's office when I got there and no one else was waiting to go in.

'Hi!' I panted, poking my head around the door.

'Oh, there you are!' said Julie, rolling her eyes.

I apologised to her and blah blah blah, and she told me not to worry and to come in and take a seat and ... (is there a law against the number of times you can say 'and' in one sentence?) there I was, sitting across from Julie Quill who was wearing her trademark low-cut top and was leaning forwards (so bulgy!) to write on her forms, and I felt extremely privileged. The sun was still shining brightly through the windows of her office, so I didn't feel too weird for keeping my sunglasses on. She continued making notes, whilst occasionally glancing up at me.

I had my head pointing slightly towards the window, so it wasn't too obvious that, behind my reflective shades, I was gawping at her bappage.

Even though I point-blank refused to believe the rumours that she'd shared those boobs (plus everything else) with Sean Palmer after last year's Christmas disco, I couldn't help imagining that there could have been a sliver of truth to it, which was ruining the moment slightly.

Has sleazy Palmer Arse-Farmer actually had a go on those? HIM? No.

It couldn't possibly be true (especially as Sean seemed to be the one spreading the rumour, and Julie isn't that kind of teacher/lady). *I severely doubt that anyone would …*

'Jaaack?' she said, not looking away from her notes.

'Juuulie?' I replied. *Juicy, juicy Julie!*

'Did you know that when the sun is shining *behind* your sunglasses, it is actually possible to see your eyes?'

BUSTED!!!

Shame. Guilt. Embarrassment. And a lot more shame.

I've been rumbled! After all these years of ogling her bust, I've finally been rumbled! On my final term of school! What the hell do I say now?!

'Aaand?' I asked, feigning both innocence and ignorance.

'Well, what exactly are you staring at so intently?' she asked, in a sing-songy voice.

Oh god, can I really deny it?

'Just trying to see what you're writing about me,' I explied, with just enough guilt thrown in to make it plausible.

'Oh, right,' she said (or possibly asked?).

She knows. She SO knows!

'OK,' she breathed chestily, whilst putting her pen down and swivelling her chair towards me. 'Let's get started.'

There was now not a single doubt in my mind that she knew. She slid her hands together, intertwined her fingers, then plunged her hands between her knees, causing her mammoth mammaries to collide in a beautiful, pink, flesh explosion.

She is testing me!

No, she's teasing me!

No, she's TORTURING me!

She can see my eyes and she is making it as hard as possible for me to not look! Do not look, Jack. Whatever you do, DO NOT LOOK!

'Oh-kaaaayyyyy,' she sighed, bending forwards slightly to glance down at my notes.

LOOK NOW!

'Film-maker . . . ' she read, snapping her eyes back up.

DON'T LOOK!

'Or writer,' she added, reading the papers again.

LOOK!

She glanced up at me.

DON'T LOOK!

'Well . . . ' she sighed, looking down again.

Oh, Jesus Christ! This is a dangerous frickin' game to play. Just look at the papers and nothing else!

And so, like the good little boy I am, I lifted my sunglasses onto my head and fixed a studious gaze upon the notes.

'You're interested in film and writing?' she checked, looking surprised.

Aaand here comes the condescending pep talk . . .

'Yeah,' I replied unashamedly.

'OK,' she continued, 'well, film and writing . . . it's . . . it's always a good idea for us to hold on to our dreams, and always strive for them, but . . . also, when thinking about your future, it's really important to remain . . . realistic, OK?'

So far, so insulting. Is she saying there's no chance I'll

157

ever make it as either of these two things? How would she know?

'We usually suggest that anyone following a path such as yours should also focus on an academic route as well, just so you have something to fall back on.'

Something to fall back on ... If I had a penny for every time a teacher told me to have something to fall back on, then I'd have ... probably about 5 or 6 p now.

'What exam subjects are you taking?' she continued, clicking her pen out and leaning forwards again.

You can keep your silly big cleavage, you creative-person hater!

(But I had a quick look anyway, just to spite her.)

Ha! I can see your boobs and I don't even care!

'Media, theatre, art and English,' I told her.

'OK! That's not too bad!' she chirped, optimistically. 'They're all quite arts-based, but English and media can open doorways towards more attainable avenues. What about ... has advertising ever taken your interest?'

What? You're supposed to be helping me achieve my career goals! Not alter them to suit you!

'Ummm,' I stalled, pretending to ponder her question, when I was in fact thinking of the best way of telling her to get lost.

But the most annoying part was that the answer was 'yes' – I have thought about a career in advertising and think it would be really good fun, but I wasn't about to admit that to her.

'I really just want to focus on something I'm passionate about,' I explained, diplomatically (or 'stubbornly', as my know-nothing mum would say).

'And so you should!' she fake agreed. 'But because they're such competitive industries, we really recommend you have something to fall back on.'

So, basically, what she was saying is that I should have something lined up for when I fail.

'I don't want to sound unsupportive, but the number of students that come through our school who want a glitzy, high-profile lifestyle, and the number of students who actually achieve that are two very different figures,' she said, gazing at me from beneath her fake-concerned brow.

Glitzy, high-profile lifestyle? It's not like I'm trying to become a pop star or a Playboy bunny! I want a career in the arts!

'Well, maybe if they weren't encouraged to focus their energy away from their interests, they might have a higher success rate,' I argued. (I'd like to say that I came up with that off the top of my head, but it was a line I'd memorised from a meeting with last year's careers advisor – but I *had* come up with it off the top of my head *then* ... just about twenty-seven minutes too late.)

Unfortunately, Julie did not find this cool in the slightest.

'Look, I'm trying to help you here,' she sigh-snapped. 'You're here for advice and that is what I'm giving you. Statistically, your desired career is highly unlikely. I'm suggesting that you aim for something with a better employment record. Whether you take that advice is entirely up to you.'

I am pleased to say that I was very polite in return and pretended to take her advice on board. Deep down inside I *know* that if I try for this, and don't stop trying, then I will get there in the end.

'So you definitely want to just focus on film or writing then?' she double-checked.

'Definitely,' I replied firmly. 'Especially as the application deadline for non-arts-related courses was three months ago,' I reminded her, making her entire argument invalid.

Ha!

'But you haven't chosen a university course yet?' she confirmed, unimpressed.

'No, sorry,' I admitted.

'Well,' she sighed, 'what about the Writing for Film BA degree at Abergavenny? Or Creative Writing for the Media at Stratford? Or . . . hang on . . . ' – she flicked through a prospectus on her PC, then – 'yeah. There's a Screenwriting course at Manchester, too?'

Oh . . . my . . . shittyknickers! How did I miss these? This is unbelievable! Writing AND film, all rolled into one! I'm applying to all three!

'Seriously?' I asked, gobsmacked.

Julie turned her monitor towards me and I spent fifteen minutes reading up on the courses, the universities, the entry requirements . . . It was almost too good to be true.

Julie handed me a folder of everything I needed to apply for the courses, which included the forms, my predicted grades and a letter of reference, which I was looking forward to reading later.

'Get these sent off no later than Monday, OK?' she ordered. 'That's the last possible day for posting. Otherwise you'll have to go through clearing. OK?'

'OK.' I smiled at my new best friend.

'And if you want me to look over your Personal

Statement, *WHEN* you've finished it, then email it to me over the weekend.'

She pushed a business card across her desk to me, which had her email and number on, then stood up to see me out.

'Good luck, Jack,' she smiled, then bent forward to give me a hug. 'Believe it or not, I might actually miss you when you're gone!' she laughed, sounding surprised. She picked up h—

Hang on. Let's go back a bit. Read that again . . .

She gave me her card with her *email* and *number* on, then she HUGGED ME!

Julie 'Big-Boobs, Hottest Teacher in the School' Quill actually HUGGED ME! I felt her lumps press against my T-shirt! Then I felt *my* lump press against my trousers!

My trousers . . . my thin-as-crap, pale khaki combat trousers . . .

Oh, nobbing frick!

JACK SAMSONITE'S PERSONAL STATEMENT: ATTEMPT #10

My name is Jack Samsonite. I grab girls' boobs. I shake wee on my trousers. And I used this application form as a penis-shield to hide my erection in front of a teacher (I get nob-ache quite a lot).

I want to do your course.

Thank you for your consideration.

<u>MY LIST OF POTENTIAL GIRLS TO GET IT ON WITH (SO FAR)</u>

1. Em (even though she's already told me she's not interested in me)
2. Edith (even though I insulted her brother and indecently assaulted her boob)
3. Sally Kirk (even though I've only ever spoken to her properly once and James fancies her)
4. Julie Quill (I can find no downside to this option. Ignore the fact that she's twice my age, she's a teacher, I find it morally abhorrent, she apparently has a boyfriend, she may or may not have had a fling with Sean Palmer and, if she did, I don't think I could ever look at her without picturing him all over her like some drooling animal, and puking ... She is really, really sexy, though!)
5. That girl who smiled at me on the bus. Oh, no, I forgot. She was laughing at my make-up. Scratch that

5. (Take two). Ummm ... anyone that'll have me, really. As long as they're nice, not a skank, pretty, classy, intelligent, considerate and preferably a non-smoking virgin

2nd PERIOD: ENGLISH WITH THE PORN STARS

Settling down in our English class and choosing not to share my horrible, Julie boob-rumble story with James, I somehow accidentally found myself in a conversation even more embarrassing.

'Are you saying you want me to show you my penis?' James asked in disgust.

'No!' I replied, and then making sure that there was no way my answer could be misconstrued to mean, 'Yes please, that would be lovely!', I reinforced this by saying, 'I do not want to see your penis!'

It was only when the rest of the class turned to give me a look of bewildered intrigue that I realised I may have said that a tad too loud.

'Great. Thanks for that,' James huffed. Then, in answer to their continued staring: 'I wasn't offering!'

'Sorry,' I grimaced, trying and failing to hide my amusement. 'I was just asking, how're you supposed to know if it's a decent size if you have no basis for reference?'

'Well ... you just know,' he shrugged, as though it

was something he has never given thought to in his entire life.

This did not make me feel better. Obviously only people with tiddly winkies ever worry about size.

I'm not sure what kind of reassurance I expected to get from James by broaching this subject. I am obviously going to have to research this for myself. (I just hope I can do it without having to form a line-up.)

Please god, don't let me have a little willy! Let it at least be average (I have a horrible feeling it's not).

'Hey, Em?' I began, my brain doing a rapid change of subject as I noticed her take the seat beside me.

I needed to know for sure whether her friend Charlie was gay or not. Her availability (or lack of) was something I needed to be sure of before I continued with my search for a get-it-on girl.

'Hey, Jack?' she replied, mimicking me.

'You know your friend, Charlie?'

Carefully, Jack! Try not to sound jealous.

'Yes,' she said, with a snigger.

Why the snigger? What does that mean?

'I think I might know him.'

'Really?' she said doubtfully, again with a snigger. 'I don't think you do.'

'Oh,' I replied. 'So it's not Camp Charlie then?'

Yes! Yes! Yes! Nice work, me!

'No,' she assured me, 'he isn't the slightest bit camp. Do you have any further questions?'

I decided I didn't want to speak to her any more.

I think that makes it official. Em is out of my life.

Just one more thing . . .

'Smudge Landen,' I told James.

'What?' he replied, as perplexed as if I'd just asked him for a kiss.

'That's my porn-star name,' I explained. 'You have to mix the name of your first pet with your mum's maiden name.'

'Yeah, I know,' he grunted. 'We did this, like, four months ago.'

Damn! His memory's normally crap!

'I don't remember,' I lied. 'What was your one?'

'Stanley Cotton,' he relented, not amused.

'Oh, yeah. No wonder I didn't remember that. Your porn star sounds like he's eighty years old and wears tweed suits.'

'Yup, that's what you said four months ago.'

Damn, damn!

Anyway, that wasn't important. That was just a warm up so it didn't sound so weird when I suddenly asked Em:

'What's your por—'

'Rusty Truncheon,' Em blurted, just as unamused as James. 'We *did* do this four months ago.'

I remember now!

'How the hell did I forget that one?' I laughed. 'That's brilliant! That is one of the . . . hang on . . . your mum's maiden name is *Truncheon*?'

Cue lots of unimportant, 'You've got the memory of a sieve' comments. They don't matter. What *does* matter is that I now have access to Em's emails. Now all I need is a computer.

3rd PERIOD: MEDIA STUDIES

After lunch, we headed to the media suite for our final lesson of the week, but there was no Ben and no sign of a substitute teacher to replace him.

'I think you should apologise to her, Jack,' said Em, as we draped ourselves lazily across the chairs.

'I did!' I protested. 'I already explained!'

'Yeah, well, not very successfully,' she scolded. 'You insult her entire family ...'

My god, how many of them have this LIC thing?!!

'You feel her tit, and you can't even say sorry?' Em continued. 'Apologise. Properly. Without using the word "retard". Before you get your invitation revoked. And this time don't make up any stupid stories about cousins that don't exist.'

She has a point. But why is she so fussed that I sleep over at Edith's? Does she want me to get it on with Edith? Or is she worried my invitation will be retracted, and then I won't be able to come out, and then she won't be able to snog me silly? Or is she just being a good friend?

'It wasn't a story! He does exist!' I insisted.

'Well ... try to make it sound less like a stupid great lie next time,' she advised, calmly. 'And do your flies up.'

It's almost as if my zipper is mocking me, mimicking my failure to progress with *anything* in my life! No matter how many times I zip myself up, I always seem to fall back down again.

My to-do list now looks something like this:

1. **Finish our short film (in order to pass my A-Levels)**
2. **Write *something* that resembles a Personal Statement in any way whatsoever!**
3. **Apply to a university (at least I know which ones to go for)**
4. **Apologise to Edith**
5. **Get in a fight**
6. **Lose my kiss-ginity to Edith. On camera. (OK, yeah, the achievability of this list is really hitting home now.)**

Screw it. Who needs a list of goals, anyway? Goals are nothing but another way to log all the things you've failed at in life. I'll just do what I do best – try to ignore my problems until they creep up on me and bite me on the balls (and hey, if that is literally what will happen if I ignore this 'get it on with Edith' problem then, as long as I catch it on camera, I can't really fail!).

I will apologise properly, next chance I get.

ON SET

There was only so long we could sit in that teacherless room before we decided to go and get on with our film. That's right, we were bunking off from our lesson to go and do work for that very same lesson. We are the goodest bad boys ever!

Even though we had no real script to speak of, and had no idea what the hell we were going to film, or who was going to star in it, we all knew exactly what we needed to film:

1. **Kisses from girls**
2. **A big action scene (preferably not too violent)**
3. **A rooftop chase.**

And since none of us had succeeded in securing me a sure kiss from a hot girl, and I had somehow so far managed to avoid getting attacked by a Jack-hating mentalist, this left us with only one thing to film. So, armed with our camera, our microphone and our trumpet (I'll explain later), we set off to nail our rooftop chase.

There was just one problem — a superhero film requires a superhero costume, and guess what we didn't have?

Lucky for us I had a plan.

MY AWESOME
PLAN TO GET US A
SUPERHERO COSTUME

There is one place in our school where costumes are readily available – the theatre. And there is only one person I know who has access to the costume room (not including teachers) – Mimi 'Mouse' Burke.

As Mimi is small, mousy and shy, I was sure that talking her into lending us some costumes would be a piece of cake. And, as if that plan wasn't awesome enough as it was, I decided we should film the whole thing. It could be like our origin story: the very first time I suit up.

'OK,' I prepped the team. 'I'll do the talking because I know what I'm talking about. I did GCSE Theatre Studies. James, you can operate the camera. Tim, you can ... just don't get in the way.'

'I'm doing music!' he protested.

'Yes. Of course. You do the music.' (Remember that trumpet?) 'I'll be all smooth and George Clooney-ish; we'll get the keys, then we can do, like, a rapid-cut montage of me suiting up, like Batman.'

'This is going to be so cool!' enthused Tim, bouncing up and down with excitement.'

'Hell, yeah, it's gonna be cool,' I assured him in my best (bad) Samuel L. Jackson impression.

Oh, yeah, it was going to be cool. Cool like one of those carrots you find at the back of your fridge, on the bottom shelf, when it's gone all soggy and bendy. Cool like a bald man's comb-over. Cool like a frickin' surprise warm turd in your ear on Christmas morning.

BRING ON THE CLOONEY

So, camera rolling, sound ... rolling too, the three of us went in search of Mimi – the girl with the key. This part was easy. As expected, Mimi was in the theatre. Time for phase two of the plan – bring on the Clooney.

This part didn't go quite to plan because, it turns out, I am about as smooth as the underside of George Clooney's little toe after he's trodden in a bowl of week-old cornflakes, then fallen asleep in the sun for eight hours.

'Hey, Mimi Mouse,' I called confidently, as I waltzed in through the theatre doors. (Clooney Cool Tip 1: If you're trying to butter someone up, it's best not to use their 'behind-their-back nickname' to their face.) Mimi stared at me, coldly.

'Can I just borrow the costume coom rey for a ... coom rey? I meant to say costume *room key*. I don't know what a coom rey is! Coom rey, it's a bit like the Welsh word for "Wales" isn't it? What is that – Cymru? Can I borrow Wales from you for a minute? Costume Wales. That doesn't even make any ... It's just ... Anyway, is it okay if I borrow the costume room key for a minute?'

Her eyes were saying 'I hate you' but I had a feeling my suave approach had won her over.

(Clooney Cool Tip 2: If you're trying to be smooth, it usually helps to plan your words beforehand, you know, to maximise flattery and minimise twattery.)

'No one's allowed the keys apart from me, and you're not even supposed to be in here, so please leave,' she replied brusquely.

Things were looking hopeful!

Then, as if possessed by Mr Smooth himself, I stepped up my game and came out with this little gem ...

'Woah! They shouldn't call you Mimi Mouse, they should call you Mimi Feisty Little ... Nob-Nugget!'

(Clooney Cool Tip 3: See Clooney Cool Tip 2.)

I *KNOW*! I have no idea where that came from! All I can say is that that sentence began with nothing but pure and complimentary intentions; the wankerishness of it was a complete accident.

'Get the hell out of my theatre, you slimy prick,' Mimi replied, clearly softening under my charm.

'Sorry,' I stuttered, 'that was supposed to ...'

'And take your arsehole friends with you,' she spat.

I'm beginning to think she might not be as shy as they say she is.

'Sorry, Mimi, I think I got off on the wrong ...' I tried to explain.

'Why are you filming me?' she demanded, noticing the camera. 'And why the hell is the creepy little one playing the trumpet?'

'Oh, yeah, we're kind of ... making a film. That's what we need the costumes for. If you could just ...'

'But why is he playing a trumpet?' she sneered, as if the very sight of Tim made her feel ill.

'He's in charge of sound and doesn't quite grasp the concept of dubbing music on afterwards,' I explained.

'That's the dumbest thing I've ever heard,' she replied, in an aggressive monotone drawl. 'He can't even play it!'

'I know,' I agreed (hey, we were finding common ground here. I was making progress!). 'But trying to talk sense to him is like . . .'

'He sounds like a cat farting in a drainpipe! What kind of film are you making?'

'It's a su—'

'I don't even care. I don't want to know. Just go. Please. Now . . . now . . . now . . . now . . .'

Something gave me the feeling she might want us to leave, but I had one last trick up my sleeve. It was a long shot, but, at this point, I had nothing to lose. I was about to make her an offer she couldn't refuse.

'We actually need someone to snog, as well,' I revealed.

THE BACK-UP PLAN

After Mimi had chased us out of the theatre, shouting threats about reporting us to the principal and stuff, I finally decided she must be a lesbian or something, so moved swiftly on to plan B.

We waited ...

We waited ...

We waited ...

Then ...

'Go! Go! Go!' I ordered.

We sprang from behind the stack of chairs in the canteen, raced towards the theatre doors, darted inside and made straight for the costume room. The camera was still rolling and Tim's nervous trumpeting was beginning to sound like an elephant having an asthma attack. Mimi had probably only left for a toilet break, which meant we only had a couple of minutes, tops.

To our amazement, the door to the costume room was unlocked. James framed the shot, I dashed inside, Tim made a noise down the trumpet that sounded like nothing on this earth, then seconds later I had an armful of costumes and we were running for our lives.

Easy as that.

Now, if I'd gone and made Plan B our Plan A in the first place, I could have saved us a lot of time. Never mind, though. What's done is done. And, more importantly, we now had an array of costumes to choose from.

THE HEIGHT OF SUCCESS

There we stood. A team of film-makers. A team of rebels. The A-Team. Rocked, locked and ready to ... no, that's not right. Whatever, we were all geared up, costumes in the bag, and ready to roll. Our first mission? Get onto the school roof.

Unfortunately, getting onto the roof isn't as easy as it sounds. The layout of our school is that we have one main building, with one huge roof (our ultimate destination), but there are about twenty different extensions built around that main building, all with their own roofs (flat ones, of course), all on different levels. So it was going to be like climbing a giant staircase to get to the top. And we were stuck at step one.

We walked round the entire circumference of the school (can a school have a circumference, or is that just for circles?) twice, before deciding that there was no possible way of making it up onto the school roof.

Tim was mindlessly babbling on about some stupid fantasy of how we could submit our film into the Short Film category of the Oscars.

'We could get some funding,' he enthused. 'Pimp it up. Get Morgan Freeman to do the voiceover, and . . .'

James came to a sudden standstill.

'SHHH!' he ordered.

We all froze. We all listened. And we all heard the same thing – voices. People were coming straight towards us from around the next corner of the building. People with voices. I spotted a small recess between the sports shed and the main school building. It was a pitiful hiding place, but it was our only option (either that, or risk getting caught skiving). The three of us huddled together in the dark little nook and watched in uncomfortable, neck-breathing-on silence as the two voices appeared around the corner and crossed in front of us.

The sight before me caused me to emit a small, involuntary groan of displeasure.

It was Letroit.

And it was Edith.

And they were *laughing together*!

I swear to god, Letroit, I will find where you live and I WILL piss in your mouthwash.

James knuckled me in the back as punishment for the noise, but I couldn't help it. I felt sick. Letroit was a student-bating paedo, and Edith was a teacher-shagging nympho. There was no other explanation. (Well, maybe there were a few other possible explanations, but none that my brain could quite grasp at that moment in time.)

OK, so maybe I was slightly overreacting. Laughing with each other doesn't necessarily *always* signify a sexual relationship but, even so, it was pretty damn sick. How could she? What could he possibly say that is even remotely amusing? She's so amazing, he's so ... twat. What is wrong with the world?!!!

Thankfully there was some good news to take my mind off that horrifying ordeal. Once the two laughing, depraved sex-fiends had rounded the next corner, I felt a tap on my shoulder. I turned to see James pointing behind us, at the only wall in school that was low enough to scale. In fact, not only was it low, but the placing of the windows and window-ledges, to use as footholds, made it so perfect I couldn't help wondering why we didn't see every idiot in school climbing up there on a daily basis.

Is it a weak roof? Is there a security camera? This should be the most popular bad-boy hangout spot in school!

Exercising extreme caution, we carefully scaled the wall and made it up onto level one. We meticulously assessed the area before moving forwards. No cameras, no holes in the roof ... nothing! Could it really be that we had found a brand-new awesome place to hang?

When we clambered up the next wall, we found the answer to that question: a great, big, resounding 'NO'.

THE HIGHER YOU CLIMB ...

There was a clear route ahead of us, one rooftop after another, none higher than six feet above the other, all very climbable (even with a video camera, a bag full of costumes and a frickin' trumpet). Except there was a problem. A BIG problem. A problem that looked distinctly like a wall of windows. And that wall of windows looked distinctly like the one that ran the length of the staff room. And that staff-roomy wall of windows was directly in front of us.

The three of us shot to the left, taking cover behind a wall. We were hidden. For now. But if we wanted to carry on going up, we were going to have to climb that window-laden wall of the staff room and, as far as I could see, there was only a two-foot portion of wall that we could possibly climb (i.e. that wasn't a window) without being seen.

It was impossible.

'Oh, well,' I sighed, 'that's that plan down the drain.'

But as I began to shuffle away, someone else spoke up. Someone I really didn't expect to say the words that were said.

'Hang on,' said James, assessing the rooftop route. 'I think we can do this.'

Great. Tim's 'stupidity' thing is catching.

And clearly it was, because, against my better judgement, I actually stuck around.

REACH FOR THE STARS

James escorted us through the 'back alleys' of the rooftop, which he assured us would lead to a section of staff-room wall that was windowless, where we would be able to climb to the next level.

'Down!' James ordered, spying Clive 'Wiggy Hair' Cornish, the science teacher, crossing the nearby staff car park towards his old yellow Toyota.

We immediately dropped, lying flat until we heard Cornish drive away. Except, when all seemed clear, and James was sprinting off around a corner, Tim remained where he was.

'Come on!' I whispered.

But he threw his hand up to silence me, then beckoned me down to where he was lying. It wasn't the most appealing of invitations until I realised where his face was situated. A narrow triangular wedge of extra roof ran the length of the girls' changing room, and a series of small, eight-inch skylight windows lined the shallow wall of the raised triangle, like large, glass letterboxes. Three of these little windows were cranked open, including the one directly in front of Tim's face.

'Watch!' he whispered, pointing in through the window.

At first there was nothing to see but, as I drew closer, the unmistakeable hiss and splat of showers peaked my interest and I had a pretty good idea of what was coming. My heart began to race.

'Shh!' he ordered, as I crouched down beside him.

I watched and waited, but still all I could see was the dividing wall of the shower room. Then, all of a sudden, Tim's breath caught in his throat and my heart did a little leap in my chest.

There was skin.

I don't know if it was an elbow or partial boob, but all I can tell you is it was chest-height, it was pale and it was triangular.

I like triangles!

It lingered there for a full two seconds before disappearing back behind the tiled wall.

Holy shit. Did I just see my first ever full-on bare boob?!

I didn't see a nipple though, and I don't think it counts if you don't see the nip (especially if it *was* an elbow). But that didn't stop my elbows from beginning to quiver.

'Ouch,' whispered Tim, adjusting something in his trouser pocket. *Oh Christ, please don't* ... 'I was doubled back on myself,' he explained. 'Nob-ache.'

I, all of a sudden, felt very ill. But, just when I thought I was ready to back away from the whole situation, an entire bare bottom revealed itself from behind the wall.

'Oh, baby!' whispered Tim.

Oh, baby?

Oh, baby?!

'Who is it?' I whispered.

'Dunno,' he replied dismissively. 'Does it matter?'

Does it ... DOES IT MATTER?!!

We're lying here, watching someone be all naked, and neither of us even knows who it is! She could be the ugliest beast in the school! She could be whale-sized! She might only be fourteen for all we know!

All of a sudden it felt really, *really* wrong. I felt like the filthiest of pervy perverts ever, and began to shuffle backwards, smoothly and quietly and desperately fast.

Unfortunately, my fastest was not quite fast enough.

THE REVELATION

Somehow, when you see it in films – a couple of kids sprawled uncomfortably across the branch of a tree, sharing a pair of binoculars whilst spying on their favourite busty neighbour – it always seems like innocent, childish fun. But when it comes to actually being a real-life voyeur, it feels kind of seedy and dirty and like a severe invasion of human rights! Except, this time, on this particular special occasion, something unbelievably mind-blowing occurred.

As I desperately began to back away from the window, despite feeling wrong for doing it I could not look away as I spied a large portion of naked hip, waist and thigh. It wasn't so much curiosity of whether I was going to see bare boob-flesh or not, but more curiosity of whose flesh I had been watching (also, a sudden, growing noise of excited girls had me feeling that there would be an entire herd of bare boobs entering that shower room the second I turned away).

First there was a foot . . .

I shuffled back further. The sound of giggling girls grew louder . . .

Then there was a calf.

I shuffled back further still ...

Then a shoulder ...

The noisy babble of boobs was surely only seconds away!

Then an arm ...

I continued to reverse ...

A buttock ...

Then ...

It all happened at once.

My dizzy, guilty, excited, conflicted brain suddenly worked it all out ... one second too late.

A thigh – a buttock – a shoulder – A PENIS!

A PENIS!

We were looking in the *boys'* changing room! That meant that the girls changing room was BEHIND ME!

Correction – BENEATH ME!

One more step back and my foot slipped straight through an open skylight window and, for one split second, my whole left leg was in the same room as an entire netball team of Year 11s. *That's* why they were getting louder – I was getting closer to *them*! How none of them noticed three feet of idiot-leg slip in and out of the shower room ceiling is a mystery. I expected to hear a chorus of screams, but all I heard was the heaving grunts of a stumbling and disoriented Tim as his disgust propelled him backwards ... and backwards ... and backwards ...

I grabbed him before he made the same leg-through-window mistake as me. But when I caught him, he reeled in surprise and ... and ...

Something touched my thigh!

I couldn't help it. I ROARED in disgust! Tim yelled in shock! Twelve naked girls screamed in horror. And two willy-spying perverts sprinted out of view of the showering girls and straight into view of a teacher-filled staff room.

THE CHASE

The screams of a dozen horrified girls caught the attention of every person in that staff room. But, before they had time to turn, I dropped behind an air-conditioning outlet and pulled Tim down with me. We were trapped. If we moved back, we would be seen through the changing-room sky-lights. If we moved forwards, we would be in full view of half the teachers in our school.

'Oh, shit!' Tim panted.

Oh, shit, indeed! We were well and truly screwed!

'Hey!' yelled a rabble of teachers, as the staff-room windows flew open. 'Get over here!/Get away from there!/Who is that?!' they all demanded at once.

And, twenty-two seconds later, Tim and I complied with every single one of those orders. We did get away from there. We did, of all places to run, go over there, and we also let them see exactly who we were ...

Goldilocks and The Gingerbread Man – our superhero alter-egos! Thinking super-fast, we'd pulled two random costumes from my bag of theatre booty (yes, my costume was The Gingerbread Man, complete with Jelly-Tot buttons, while Tim was Goldilocks, complete with frock, wig and heels) and we masked our identities like true masters of disguise.

I didn't know how he had done it, but James was already there, up on the roof, lying, unseen, directly above the room full of yelling teachers. And ...

No. Shitting. Way ...

He was filming the whole thing!

At first I wasn't sure if Tim had spotted him, but when I heard the telltale sounds of an imbecile blowing raspberries down a trumpet, I knew it was happening. We were well and truly making a film unlike any other. And, even though I was *this* close to letting that imprisoned poo straight out of my petrified bottom, I couldn't help but laugh.

JACK SAMSONITE: THE MOVIE

EXT. ROOFTOP — DAY

The one dressed as a large biscuit is
gradually breaking away from the short one in
the dress and blonde wig, who bravely attempts
to resuscitate the trumpet that wails in agony
in his arms.

The mob of hungry flesh-eaters claw their
gnarled and decaying arms through the small
openings of the child-proof safety windows.
Desperate to break free of their coffee-
stinking enclosure, they clutch and clasp at
the clothing of the biscuit-boy and the little
drag-queen, who attempt to make it up onto the
roof, aided by their camera-wielding
accomplice.

Jack The Biscuit breathes a sigh of relief
as he watches James pull Timmylocks up to
safety. This is closely followed by a breath
of terror as he looks back down and sees
something truly horrifying — a key. His legs
scramble desperately for purchase on the
slippery windowpane as he watches the key
being inserted into a window lock by one of
the larger brain-dead.

The window opens.

One leg steps out.

Then another.

A moment later and there he is, in all his hulking great glory — Letroit the French Nazi Zombie is just a few feet from Jack The Biscuit and he is ready to eat.

James turns his head away, so as not to be identified.

JAMES

Take my hand!

Jack The Biscuit doesn't need telling twice. Letroit the French Nazi Zombie dashes for Jack's legs. His fingers close around a swatch of crusty, crap-covered trouser leg, then, in a flash, his prey is gone. James hauls his friend to safety, and the three of them lie there for a moment, catching their breath, until they see it — the great, hulking beast is clawing his way up.

JACK

RUUUUUUUUUUUUNNNNNNNNNNN!!!!!!!!!!!

The trio of desperados hurl themselves into a sprint across the rooftop. Letroit follows in hot pursuit. Timmylocks tails James as he breaks left. Jack The Biscuit, unaware of their departure, continues straight ahead. So does Letroit.

Gingerbread Jack is only aware of his

solitude when he reaches the edge of the rooftop. He looks desperately around for his accomplices, but he is all alone, bar the gigantic great beast bearing down on him. Ahead is nothing but air. And beneath that air — a good twenty feet below — is the ground. He takes a moment to weigh up his options.

Behind him — Letroit.

In front — the drop.

Letroit.

The drop.

He opts for the lesser of the two evils.

He jumps.

MY DOWNFALL

OK, so maybe it was more like fifteen feet, not twenty. And maybe I didn't exactly 'jump', but carefully lowered myself down until my feet were as close to the ground as possible. But still, it was very high and very scary and, despite my cautious descent, I still managed to sustain a horrific injury.

I ran, in a slightly skewed straight line, across the bus bay and towards the back of school, my hand clutched firmly over my wound. I glanced over my shoulder to gauge Letroit's progress. He was at the edge of the roof and, to my great relief, that was apparently where he was going to stay. (I don't blame him. If he had jumped, he'd have been faced with the task of climbing out of the crater he'd have created on impact.)

I hope you get stuck up there, you Edith's-laugh-extracting sicko!

Relaxing slightly in my new, unhunted state, I paused to assess the damage. I pulled my hand away from my stinging eye and, to my horror, saw blood trickling down my sacrifice finger, and felt the warm, wet, blood-soaked fabric of my Gingerbread mask clinging to my face.

It hadn't seemed too bad at the time. Just a little nick as I had lowered myself down the wall and caught the corner of my eye on the non-dangerous end of a protruding screw. It can't have been a big cut, but there was a lot of blood.

Suddenly I panicked. A lot of blood! Around my eye!

It wasn't the fact that I'd sustained an injury that had me worried; it was the fact that Letroit had *seen*! He'd watched as I dabbed at my bleeding eye. He knew, and I knew, that, like a bank robber stained by a dye pack, I was a marked man.

I turned and ran – a brand-new fear giving me flight.

JACK SAMSONITE'S PERSONAL STATEMENT: ATTEMPT #11

My name is Jack Samsonite and I am a criminal. I snuck out of my media lesson, I stole a gingerbread-man costume, I spied on a naked guy in the shower, I poked my leg into a room full of naked girls, and now I am a fugitive on the run from an oversized French Nazi Zombie who is currently stranded on the roof of the school gym. And that's just the past hour!

As you can see, I am in desperate need of a proper education. Please help.

MY ONLY HOPE

A quick trip to the boys' toilets confirmed my fear – I was cut. It wasn't a huge gash, but it was big enough to spot if you knew what you were looking for. And Letroit would know exactly what to look for.

There was only a select number of people who could help me. They were my only hope. With my 'superhero' costume stowed back in my bag, I went in search of salvation.

The bell rang for final break. Now was my moment. I casually breezed out of the toilets and disappeared into the deluge of bodies that spilled from the classrooms and flooded the corridors. After five minutes of scouring the hallways for one of the faces of my salvation, I finally gave up and left the building in search of James and Tim. And then I saw them. My angels. All three of them, together, disappearing around the corner of school and towards the playing field.

'Em!' I called. 'Guys! Wait up!'

There are very few pressures as pressy as walking towards three very pretty girls, who are all watching and waiting for you, and may or may not love/hate you. It's these kinds of pressures that make me very conscious of how I walk.

How DO my legs know to put one foot in front of the other without me ever having to tell them?

(This was the point where the above phenomenon ceased to exist, and I had to remind my legs of how to do their job.)

Crap. Am I walking funny now? Are they all looking at me, observing how strange my walk is?

(This was the point where I tried to make my forced walk look unforced, resulting in me resembling a *Thunderbirds* puppet.)

Christ, I must look like a freak! Stop thinking about it! And what do I do with my arms? Do I swing them? Do I stuff them in my pockets? How do normal people walk? Is it weird that I'm looking at them? Should I look around a bit? Lift your feet. Swing your arms. Check out those clouds. Try not to . . .

(And this was the point that I hit a ditch and fell flat on my face.)

'Come onnnn!' moaned Em, with a smirk. 'We're waiting! Why do you always have to play the fool?'

That's right! Yes! I did it all on purpose! I was just pre-tending to be an idiot!

'Sorry!' I laughed stupidly, possibly giving away the truth about my idiotness.

I decided that this would be a good time to fumble for my sunglasses in my bag. Not only would they eliminate the whole 'Where do I look?' dilemma, but they would also hide the eye scratch.

'We're actually trying to discuss our Science project here Jack,' Em informed me.

I paused.

Does this mean they want me to leave?

'Hurry up then, if you're coming!' Em groaned again, like an impatient big sister (another reminder that she has lost any romantic interest in me).

I quickly broke into a jog and immediately tripped over again, but heroically managed to steady myself before actually hitting the ground.

Frickin' crap!

'Right. That's it. Come on,' Em instructed the other two, who were laughing. 'We've got better things to do than watch you toss about like Charlie-bloody-Chaplin!'

Edith is laughing?

Edith is laughing?

Does she like me again now? I thought I was an 'obnoxious idiot'. And I grabbed her boob. And I said 'retard'. Twice. And I never really did apologise properly! But she hasn't revoked my sleepover invitation. Yet. Maybe she does like me! Or maybe she just takes pleasure in seeing me hurt myself. Girls are stupid! Not that I care. Teacher-tramp.

'Come on, you big idiot,' laughed Sally, reaching a hand out for mine, as Em impatiently walked ahead.

Sally wants to hold my hand?

'That last fall really was an accident!' I admitted (as if the first one wasn't).

And then – to my hugest of surprises – as I took Sally's hand in my left one, Edith's hand took hold of my right one!

'Do you need us to look after you?' Edith cooed, like she was talking to a baby.

She's talking to me? She's <u>touching</u> me! I don't get it!

'Yes, I do,' I said (secretly talking to an invisible camera, with a raised eyebrow).

Ergh. Sometimes I creep myself out! Don't do that again.

'Awww, diddums!' said Sally, wrapping her arms around my left one.

Is she ...

Was she?

Are <u>they</u> ...?

Were they?!

I think they might be ...

Were they *flirting* with me?!!

Maybe I was wrong about the whole teacher-tramp thing?

I decided to give Edith the benefit of the doubt.

'You can stop blushing, Jack,' said Em, spinning round with a tired expression on her face. 'They're not flirting with you, they just think you're a fool.'

Oh. Really?

Sally looked at me apologetically and shrugged.

'It's true,' she giggled.

And then they laughed. And laughed. And laughed ...

I don't care, because, even though it's kind of tame, I think this is a Jack Sandwich!

'Sorry for not believing you,' Edith said quietly, once she'd finished laughing.

'About what?' I asked.

'Your cousin,' she admitted.

My cousin? What about my cousin?

'Huh?' I queried.

'I ...' she paused, looking ashamed about something. 'I saw you helping him off the bus this morning,' she explained.

It took a moment, but finally ...

'Oh! My *cousin*!' I clarified. 'Ass-burgers! My cousin, Ass-burgers, with the big orange afro,' I nodded, finally realising what the hell was happening here, and mimicking his stampy-feet, face-on-his-shoulders, hobble-in-circles reaction to getting gum in his eye.

She thinks Pumpkin is my re-cousin!

The bloody genius!

'I had no idea it could get that bad,' she said softly, with sympathetic eyes.

'Yeah, it ... wait, you didn't believe me?' I frowned, feigning insult at the idea that I might have made the whole thing up.

'I guess I have some trust issues,' she shrugged. 'Sorry.'

In time I would learn to forgive her.

I can't believe this!

All of a sudden, in her mind, our roles had completely reversed! I was now the good guy and she felt like the bad guy, all thanks to Pumpkin getting spat on.

OK, so ... getting Edith to not hate my guts – done (with surprisingly little effort!). Now all that remained was to ask one of these girls to put ladies' make-up on my face whilst keeping my super-cool heterosexual macho man reputation intact.

Could be tricky, especially as the sight ahead of me now had me flustered beyond belief: Sean Palmer had appeared from somewhere, caught up with Em, and the two of them were looking very friendly indeed.

ASKING A GIRL TO WORK ON MY FACE

I wasn't too sure why we were going up the field. No one really goes up the field any more. Not since they built a sports store room on Metaller's Corner at least (that was our old hangout). People *spill onto* the field from the playground, but only the stoners, super-young smokers and the hardcore heavy-petters actually bother to venture to the far end.

Hmmmm, the hardcore heavy-petters ... was Sean Palmer's appearance just a coincidence, or was it planned? Whose idea was it to come up here?

It seemed that Sally wasn't too sure why we were up there, either.

'Why are we even going up the field, anyway?' she asked.

'Dunno,' said Em.

Edith gave a shrug.

'Can we like, stop? Only my feet are killing in these shoes!' Sally winced.

'And this new bag's really cutting into my shoulder,' complained Edith.

'Yeah,' said Em, instantly dropping to the ground, legs crossed.

'What is it with girls and shoes?' I asked, as my hands were released and the rest of us sat down. 'If a guy buys shoes, the first thing he does is make sure they're comfortable!'

'Bullshit!' said Em, defensively. 'Tim spent ninety quid on a pair of Nikes! Are you telling me he bought them for comfort over style?'

'Yeah, well, Tim doesn't count,' I replied. 'Tim isn't a *guy*, he's a genetic freak of nature.'

Sean remained uncharacteristically quiet. When I noticed his polished, bank-manager-style kipper-shoes, I realised why.

Ha! You expensive-shoe-buying fool!

Now do something to overthrow his fake nice-boy act. Let them see just how nice he isn't.

'Here,' I said, holding my opened bag towards Edith. 'Stick your bag in there, if you like. I'll carry it for you.'

'Aww, thank you!' she cooed, slipping her small but heavy purse thing into it.

Her bag is in my bag!

(It excited me. I can't explain it.)

My insides went strangely warm and gooey, then quickly hardened when I saw Em and Sally share a look of raised eyebrow amusement.

What am I doing? Keep your options open! Be nice to everyone! And ... oh, this could be good ...

'Anyone else want me to carry anything?' I offered, holding out my bag and trying not to sound weird.

Please Em, say 'yes', then give me your bag and your phone, so that I can tamper with your emails. Do it!

'Er, you're all right, thanks,' and 'I'm fine,' they responded, acting as weirdly as if I'd just asked if I could inspect the fit of their bras.

Are girls' bags sacred artefacts? Did I just do something weird?

Sean shuffled into a comfier position, then cleared his throat, as if getting ready to speak.

No! Don't let it happen!

I couldn't let Sean take to the stage. He'd start on one of his epic tales, steal my limelight, soak up everyone's attention.

Beat him to it! Think of something to talk about! Something awesome ... something gripping ... something totally compulsive ...

And then it clicked. A conversation I had heard once before ... the most compelling debate known to man ... it couldn't fail ...

'So ...' I sighed, relaxing in the knowledge that I had struck conversational gold, 'I don't know about you guys, but I wipe my bum *sitting down*.'

Everyone stopped. Everyone stared. A tumbleweed blew between us. It hadn't worked quite as I'd planned. And it reminded me that I needed to poo.

'Oh, Christ,' groaned Em, 'if you're going to start this sit down/stand up conversation then I think I'd rather go to the library.'

'I'll come, too!' Sean added, way too quickly.

Then the two of them got up and left. Just like that.

That . . .

Was not . . .

Supposed to happen.

LAST BREAK: THREE
BECAME TWO

If Em telling me 'I think this is a mistake' two years ago wasn't a big enough sign that we're never going to get it together, then her disappearing to the library with Sean Palmer pretty much hammered the final nail in the coffin of all my hopes and dreams.

'Do you think they're going to read something in the philosophy section?' Edith whispered. 'Something *deep* and *penetrating!*'

The thought made me feel instantly ill (which was swiftly remedied when Edith sprawled herself out and rested her head on my lap).

Holy crap! I just totally bypassed the 'bums-on-laps' phenomenon and jumped straight to FACES on laps! This is AMAZING! (A little too *amazing . . . ?)*

Edith: 1 Sally: 0

'Oh my god, don't even go there,' Sally groaned. 'That would be the biggest mistake of her life.'

'You really don't like him, do you?' Edith gaped in disbelief.

'I can't stand the slimy git!' Sally sneered.

Edith: 1 Sally: 1

'Awww, I think he's sweet!' Edith cooed, in Sean's defence.

Sally: 1 Edith: minus 200 . . .

And then, as part of her cooing, she unconsciously curled her fingers around the underside of my thigh, as if I was a pillow.

Edith: 482!!!!!

This was amazing! She invited me around for a sleepover, and now she's using me as a pillow! I so hope she continues to use me as bedding this evening!

And then I remembered . . .

Pale . . .

Thin . . .

Combats!

THIN!!!

This was one time in my life when I *didn't* need my nob to look any bigger than it was.

Edith . . . whatever you do . . . do not move your head!

There was a snake in my pants and it was slowly edging her way!

Distract it! Distract the snake! Think of ugly people! Andrew Lloyd Webber! Picture him!

It was no use; even Andrew Lloyd Webber is no match for a real girl's face.

Picture him naked! Splashing in mud! Wearing lederhosen!!

It was working! Andrew Lloyd Webber had scared the snake into a standstill.

Keep going! More ugly! Go, go, go!

But before I even began to picture Barry Manilow in a leotard, Edith went and ruined everything by humming a Beatles song.

No! Stop it! Stop the vibrations! It feels NICE!

Think ugly! NOW! Before she meets MY Yellow Submarine!

What was wrong with me? There she was, being all nice and lovely and snuggly, and I was going to repay her by stabbing her in the ear with my willy!

'Who was your biggest mistake?' Edith asked Sally.

Yes! No more humming! Talk. Let's have a conversation . . .

'You mean like . . . ?'

'Worst shag ever,' Edith clarified.

'Oh god, errr . . . '

How is she struggling with an answer? How many bad shags has she had?

But it was good. It was working. The snake was feeling ill.

'Mark Jacobs,' Sally finally decided, with no shadow of a doubt. 'My first time . . . '

OK, don't need to know the details. Picturing you with other men? Not good.

But it *was* good. The snake was slowly becoming a worm once more.

'Oh god, he was disgusting!' she continued.

Erghh! I don't want to know!

Sally: minus 324

'All right, that'll do,' groaned Edith, adjusting herself on my thigh and squeezing tight.

No! No! Do not wake the snake!

'What about you, then?' Sally asked Edith.

Whatever it was, it was in danger of being trumped by that time, up the field, when Jack Samsonite accidentally sexed her in the ear . . .

'We'll come back to that,' Edith quickly replied. 'I want to know about Jack's!'

'Yesssss!' agreed Sally.

Oh, dear.

'Ummmmm . . .'

Nervousness. Yes, nervousness is good! Nervous thinkings make willy shrinkings.

'Too many to choose from?' Edith asked.

'Nnnnot . . . quite,' I accidentally admitted.

Edith suddenly sat bolt upright. Her face was horror-stricken.

Oh, dear . . .

She looked horribly like someone who had just experienced an acute attack of nob-in-ear syndrome!

No!

It was . . .

'I . . .' I tried to explain.

'Are you a *virgin*?' she asked in utter surprise.

THANK GOD!

'Ummmmmm . . .'

'Oh my god!' squealed Sally, clapping her hands together.

'That is *so* cute!' Edith sighed, surveying me like I was a cuddly puppy.

'I can't believe that!' Sally shook her head in disbelief.

Because I'm super-hot, or because you've been doing it since you were twelve?

'Right,' said Edith, pointing a finger at me, 'you are *so* getting laid tonight. I'm going to make sure of it.'

Wha ...?

Edith:1000000000000000000000000000000000000000000000
000000000000000000000000000000000000000000000000000000
000000000000000000000000000000000000000000000000000000
000000000000000000000000000000000000000000000000000000
000000000000000000000000000000000000000000000000000000
000000000000000000000000000000000000000000000000000000
000000000000000000000000000000000000000000000000000000
000000000000000000000000000000000000000000000000000000
000000000000000000000000000000000000000000000000000000
000000000000000000000000000000000000000000000000000000
000000000000000000000000000000000000000000000000000000
000000000000000000000000000000000000000000000000000000
000000000000000000000000000000000000000000000000000000
000000000000000000000000000000000000000000000000000000
000000000000000000000000000000000000000 and two!

3rd PERIOD: MEDIA STUDIES (AGAIN)

I think that's pretty much confirmed: tonight, for the first time ever, I shall waggle my willy in a woo-woo (that sounds more disturbing than it did in my head). Maybe 'willy' and 'woo-woo' aren't appropriate words for someone my age. How about this: I am going to waggle my penis in a vagi . . . no, I think that's worse. Maybe it was the word 'waggle' that did it? Tonight, for the first time ever, I shall poke my plunger into a pretty girl's pu. . ? How are you supposed to say this without it sounding messed up? Am I going to have to be all conservative and coy and say things like, 'I shall be inserting my P into a lady's V'? Jesus, no. That's the worst one of all!

Hey! Look! I can't believe I've never noticed this before, but if you put your dirty eyes in and look at the letter 'P', it looks a bit like a droopy nob and a ball from the side! Seriously! And if you look at the letter 'V', it looks a bit like a lady-muff triangle thing! This is awesome! Has anyone else ever figured this out, or have I stumbled on something groundbreaking here? I think I might be a proper genius!

How many other words begin with a letter that looks like the object it's describing? 'Orange' – there's one. 'Snake'. 'Boobs' – hey, that's a double whammy because not only does the 'B' look like a sideways pair, but the 'oo' looks pretty good, too! It must go on and on! I think I've invented a whole new code language here. Now, whenever I read the word 'Oops', all I'll be able to see is, 'Orange orange penis snake'! But I fear I may be rambling . . .

Getting back to reality . . . The bell for third period had actually rung a long while ago, but as long as Sally and Edith weren't going anywhere, then neither was I. Besides, it's not like I was skiving; I was laying the groundwork for the most vital scene of our film. I was on the way to securing a kiss (or maybe even more than that if Edith keeps to her word!) for this evening and I knew it.

Then, just when I thought I was making progress, Sally goes and spoils it all by saying something stupid like, 'We should really go and find Em and make sure Sean Palmer isn't trying to get her pregnant or anything.'

Talk about putting a downer on things!

So they went off to find Em, I went off to find my film crew (who, it had only just occurred to me, could still be on the roof or, even worse, could've been captured!). I rushed back to the media suite, entered our second teacherless media lesson of the afternoon and there they were, watching the incriminating rooftop footage on the digital projector.

'Are you insane?' I barked, as I checked the room to make sure they were alone.

'Where the hell did you disappear to?' asked James, accusingly.

'Who, me?' I asked, taking offence at his tone. 'Oh, I just got chased down by that big great oaf, hurled myself off a thirty-foot-high roof, and got a nail in my eye for my troubles!'

Shit. My eye! I totally forgot to ask the girls to cover it up!

'Oh,' was James's reply.

'Where have *you* been?' I asked, sounding like I'd been searching for them non-stop.

'Here,' was James's reply.

'Oh,' was my reply. 'Doing what?'

'This ...' said James, pointing to the film that was being projected onto the wall.

The extremely shaky, hand-held-camera footage showed me sprinting along the rooftop, away from Letroit, then Tim running in front of the camera and blocking the shot.

JACK SAMSONITE: THE MOVIE

Cut to: -

EXT. SOME WALL SOMEWHERE, WHICH IS OBVIOUSLY
SUPPOSED TO BE ON THE ROOF, BUT CLEARLY ISN'T
BECAUSE THERE'S A BIN IN SHOT — DAY.

Timmylocks runs into shot, fake-breathless, as
though fresh from fleeing Letroit, grinds to a
halt, then begins talking into his watch.

> TIMMYLOCKS
> Mummy Bear, this is the Blond Avenger,
> come in. I repeat, Mummy Bear, this is the
> Blond Avenger, come in! Over.

A voice replies from his watch (but sounds
suspiciously as if it might actually be coming
from someone behind the camera, talking into
their sleeve).

> MUMMY BEAR/WATCH
> Blond Avenger, this is Mummy Bear, I read
> you loud and clear. What is your situation?

> BLOND AVENGER/TIMMYLOCKS
> Our situation is very, very ... dodgy. The
> Masked Assassin has sent one of his
> henchmen to take us down. We need back-up.

```
            I repeat, we need back-up! Urgently! Now!
            Please!


                     MUMMY BEAR/WATCH
            What does the henchman look like, Blond
            Avenger?


     Blond Avenger stares off-screen, and dramatic
     horror washes over his face.


                  BLOND AVENGER/TIMMYLOCKS
            He's gigantuan, chalkasian, bespoke, brown
            haired.


                     MUMMY BEAR/WATCH
            Sit tight, Blond Avenger, I'm on my way ...
```

'Woah,' I said, picking up the remote control and pausing
the footage. 'What the hell is it that you think "bespoke"
actually means?'

'Duh!' said Tim, as if I were an idiot for not knowing. 'It
means "wearing spectacles", you div! Get an education.'
And with that, he snatched the controls from my hand and
the movie masterpiece was rolling once more.

```
     Blond Avenger looks up into the sky. He
     squints, as though trying to focus on
     something distant. A sound, not unlike James's
     mouth making the noise of an approaching jet
     plane, grows louder and louder. Blond
```

Avenger's head slowly turns, as though
tracking something up in the sky. He takes a
step back, then ...

BAM! Mummy Bear (James in a big teddy-bear
costume) jumps into shot. I mean, he lands on
the rooftop, then runs off in the supposed
direction of the henchman. The camera stays
put. There are lots of grunts, crashes and
yelps and the occasional piece of debris flies
across the shot. Blond Avenger winces and
ducks as he looks on at what can be nothing
less that total bloody carnage.

Mummy Bear finally returns into shot, looking
behind him.

                    MUMMY BEAR
   Take that, you henchman! And don't come
   back!

The screen turns to white-noise.

James and Tim sat there, smugly awaiting my appraisal of
their movie-making initiative.
   There was only one thing to say.
   'What the shitty penguins was *that*?'

AT LONG LAST ...

James and Tim began to explain how they had managed to produce such a glorious film-making turd in such a short space of time, and were clearly waiting for me to tell them how impressed I was (which wasn't going to happen).

'Sooo ...' James stretched, looking uncomfortable about something.

'Soooo?' I echoed.

'Obviously we still need a *real* fight,' he explained.

'Obviously,' I agreed, 'because that wasn't quite, entirely, one hundred per cent *documentary style*, was it?'

'And we're still waiting for that kiss ...' James continued, glossing over my last comment, 'which I've been meaning to talk to you about. You see ...'

But, before he had a chance to get whatever it was he clearly wanted to get off his chest, he was interrupted by someone behind me entering the media suite.

Tim's jaw dropped.

James's eyes bulged.

219

This had to be one seriously hot girl (or at least one seriously good cleavage show).

I lazily turned around to see what poor young lady had fallen victim to the 'piece of meat' greet of the idiot twins, and immediately realised my mistake.

This was no girl.

This was Letroit's butt.

And it was not hot.

He groaned in pain as he bent to lower his bag to the floor, and I sprang into action. Whilst he had his back to me I whipped the camera from the desk beside me, held it to my eye to cover the injury, then, just as he began to turn, I swiped the incriminating blond wig from Tim's head and prayed to god that all evidence of our wrong-doing was now out of sight. Because if it wasn't, we were well and truly screwed.

The three of us were now face to face with the henchman, doing our best to act natural, and all awaiting the bollocking of a lifetime.

'And how many hours a week would you say you spend doing homework?' I asked James, as if we were halfway through an interview.

'Err ... twenty?' James replied nervously.

Twenty?

'And which subject would you say you focus most of your ...'

'Hello,' Letroit growled, rudely interrupting our fake filming.

I stopped and turned, making sure to keep the camera pressed over my damaged eye.

'Hi,' I replied nervously.

'Can I ask what you're doing?' he said, a shallow ebb of anger threatening to break his cold, still surface.

'Oh, we're filming a documentary about a week in the life of an A-level student,' I explained, possibly a tad too nicey-nicely. 'We're all filming today,' I quickly added, making sure he knew that we wouldn't be the only bunch of students hanging round with a video camera (which we probably were, since everyone else had probably finished their films and handed them in for marking days ago). 'The deadline's Monday.'

'Oh,' he replied.

And then he stared.

We stared back.

Silence stared at all of us.

Letroit locked on to the camera.

I locked on to him.

Poo locked on to my sphincter.

He's going to ask me to put it down. I know he is! What the hell am I going to do?!!!

He finally spoke.

'Eye . . .'

'No!' I pleaded without even thinking.

'No what?' he frowned, anger cracking his brow.

It suddenly dawned on me that he may have actually said 'I' and not 'Eye'.

'Eye . . . I don't know. Sorry, I . . .'

SHUT UP!

'I . . . don't suppose you know where everyone else is filming, do you?' he continued.

PHEW!

221

'Ummm ...' I replied, wishing James or Tim would muster the testicles to help me out at some point.

'Only I'm accustomed to having students in the classes I teach.'

That YOU teach? He's our substitute teacher?

'Well, perhaps if you had showed up at the <u>start</u> of the lesson ...' is exactly what I did not say to him.

'Yeah, no,' I squirmed, shrinking beneath his accusing stare, 'I don't know.'

'Any of them in fancy dress?' he asked, causing me to break into a hot sweat in an instant.

'I don't know,' I repeated. 'Costumes are more of a theatre studies thing, I think.'

Yes! Nice one! Throw him off the scent! Send him sniffing elsewhere!

'And do they usually use video cameras in theatre studies?' he asked, his suspicion adding a lilt of sarcasm to his voice.

James and Tim both suddenly chose this exact moment to begin talking.

'Yes!' they stupidly blurted, much too loudly and way too fast ... ly.

'Sometimes,' I quickly corrected them, in an attempt to mask their blatant guilt, before adding the stupidest word I could have possibly chosen ... 'Why?'

Once again he stared.

Once again I stared back.

The camera over my eye was beginning to feel like a huge elephant in the room. I had a horrible feeling something bad was about to happen.

222

'Anyway,' said Tim, with an assertive tone of authority, 'we really need to go and interview a teacher before the end of the lesson.'

What is he doing?!!

Letroit's glare shifted from me and settled on Tim.

'Well, don't look at me,' he said, carefully lowering himself into a seat, keeping his right leg straight and wincing in pain (had he jumped off the roof, after all?). 'Try the staff room,' he added. 'There're plenty of them up there.'

Tim, you're a bloody genius!

'OK,' said Tim, struggling to hide the relief in his voice. 'Thanks!'

And, with that, we began to leave the room, barely believing we had got away with it and desperately trying to get out of there as fast as we could, in the calmest way possible, before he pinned us down with a question that we *couldn't* answer.

Go!

We shuffled across the room.

Go! Go!

We opened the door.

Go! Go! Go!

We stepped outside.

Yes!

We were free!

'Hold on!' Letroit called.

Noooooooo!

We shuffled back into the doorway. Letroit pulled something from his bag.

'Any of you know who this belongs to?'

It glistened in his hand, light bouncing off every inch of its shiny surface, all except for the small, white, name-tag sticker that sat in the trumpet's funnel, reading: 'Tim Suchton'.

LETROIT HAS THE HORN

If Letroit hadn't seen the name-tag, then we certainly weren't going to point it out to him. After a chorus of 'no's and a sway of headshakes, Letroit dismissed us once more. Only, this time, we didn't feel quite so elated.

'Tim?' I asked, as we trudged away from the media suite, moving like three criminals making our final walk from Death Row, 'did you, by any chance, drop your trumpet on the school roof?'

Tim made no attempt at answering. He stared unblinkingly at the ground, in a semi-catatonic state.

'Only, because, if you did,' I continued, 'I think I know where it is.'

'We are so screwed,' muttered James.

'Yes, we are,' I agreed, knowing it would only be a matter of time before Letroit discovered Tim's name on the trumpet, and would then link him to us, his film-making partners. There was no way we would get away with this one. No way *I* would get away with this one. Not after yesterday's 'vagina' comment. 'Unless . . .'

*

It all started so smoothly. The media suite was still empty except for Letroit, who was sitting at Ben's desk, messing about on his phone. I had drawn the short straw, so James and Tim went in first. A few seconds later, the two of them were in the camera store room with Letroit. Then it was my turn. I slipped in silently. I rummaged through his bag – no trumpet. I searched the desk – no trumpet. I scoured the entire room, and then . . .

'Ah, you're big lads, you don't need my help,' I heard Letroit say, before he hobbled out of the store room.

No! Balls!

I did the superhero thing and quickly hid under the desk. That was a very, very, bad, bad move. Not only do people with sprained ankles not wish to help James and Tim lift heavy things from high shelves in the store room but, it turns out, they also like to sit down a lot. And sit down he did.

It was a proper desk, the bureau kind, with drawers on both sides and a backboard thing (which is clearly designed to stop pesky students from fleeing their hiding place).

Either that, or it's for hiding teachers' nob-aches.

(Aaaaaand there was the worst image of the day.)

Letroit placed something heavy and trumpet-sound-alikey on the desk, gave his ankle a firm rub, then pulled his chair in. RIGHT in! It took super-fast, super-silent, super-human reactions to spread my legs around his feet, then press the back of my head into the underside of the desk drawer as his nuts came rushing towards my face.

It was hell.

I heard James wander in, then pause and say, 'OK, erm . . . see ya.' Then he left. They left! They left me there all alone!

Now I know what it must be like for people with locked-in syndrome. I was desperate to call James's name, to scream for help, but I couldn't speak. I couldn't move! Hell, I could barely breathe for fear that he might feel my breath on his balls!

Oh, Christ ... if he gets even a mild *case of nob-ache right now, his penis will actually be in my face!*

I focused all my energy on using The Force to call James back.

I'm under the desk! Come back! Come baaack!

But my cries for help went unheard: he had set sail for dry land and I was going to slowly and silently slip away, never to be seen again. There was no way James could have known I was down there, with a penis in my nose. He probably thought I was waiting outside for him somewhere. But he wouldn't be able to find me. And then he'd ...

My phone! It isn't on silent! He's going to phone me to see where I am! I have to ...

By this point, the muscles at the back of my knees, under my thighs and up my back were all screaming for release, trembling under the strain of sitting like a contortionist. And, on top of that, I had to remove one of my supporting hands from the floor and try to slip my phone from my pocket.

There were just two problems with this:

1. **98 per cent of my concentration was focused on not letting my head sink into Letroit's crotch**
2. **When you're bent 90 degrees at the waist and practically doing the splits, it has a way of**

> *closing* **your pockets, making it near impossible
> to slide *anything* out.**

My panicked fingertips fumbled feverishly at the opening to my pocket, but they couldn't find their way in.

Get it! Get the damn phone before it rings!

I tried not to picture what would happen if my stupid Abba ringtone blasted out from beneath the desk, but I couldn't help it. Not only would Letroit find me with my face in his nuts, but he would also get a very clear view of the incriminating scratch on my eye, which would all contribute to my parents receiving the world's most embarrassing expulsion letter: 1. Mum's vagina 2. Gingerbread man 3. Girls' shower room 4. Nut sniffing ...

My fingers finally found my pocket opening, then the smooth, hard corner of my phone. I clasped it tight and began to pull with all my mighty fingertip strength. It took every ounce of super-neck power to keep nose from nads, but luckily the repulsion factor gave me extra strength from deep, untapped reserves that I hadn't known existed. (You know how they dangle carrots in front of horses to encourage them to move forwards? Well, they could do a similar thing for rickshaw drivers, except, instead of dangling a carrot in front, they could dangle Letroit's chubby genitals behind.)

The phone was almost out. One last tiny pull slid it straight from my compressed pocket and into my hand. I fumbled for the 'Silent' switch and, as I did, the screen lit up.

Someone was calling, but I couldn't see who! My phone

was hurt. I must have damaged it in the rooftop chase: the screen was cracked and bleeding black blood across the top of the screen. I slammed that silent switch across as fast as I could, cutting the ringtone off before it had a chance to start. The phone acknowledged my request with a gentle vibration and a barely audible 'Vvvvvvp'.

Letroit froze.

He heard that?

I held my breath.

My heart began head-butting my ribs.

Then ...

Letroit continued messing with his phone.

That was close.

My desperation to speak to James caused me to press 'Answer', even though I knew I couldn't talk. I think I was hoping that he might listen very carefully and maybe spot some telltale sounds that would direct him to underneath the desk in the media suite.

As it happens, there is very little to hear between Letroit's legs. At least there *was* ...

'HELLO?' the tinny voice was emitted from the earpiece at a surprisingly audible volume! 'HELL—'

End Call! END CALL!

Letroit froze again. This time for a far more torturous length of time.

Don't look under the desk. Do NOT look under the desk!

He began to move slightly.

No ...

He shuffled in his seat.

Stay!

He lifted one buttock . . .

PLEASE!!!

And once again the below-desk silence was shattered.

His rumbling fart resonated through the air with such a deep tremor that I'm almost certain it made my lips vibrate.

Oh, Christ! GO! PLEASE! Go!!!

Life always has a funny way of reminding you that, no matter how bad things might seem, it can always be worse. I just wish life would attempt teaching theory rather than always resorting to practical.

Stupid life!

I don't think I need to elaborate on how frickin' repulsed I was right then: as if the picture wasn't bad enough, he had to go and throw in surround-sound and smell-o-vision. I could hear him tinkering on his phone again, and prayed to god that he wasn't looking at porn.

The last thing I need is to see this in 3D!

I held my breath and wasted no time in blindly texting my reply to the text that I knew James would inevitably be sending me.

'*Inder the dwaj!*' (Obviously, I wasn't aware of how badly misspelled it was at the time.)

And, as I predicted, in came his question, just as I was sending my pre-emptive reply.

'*Where are you?*'

He would come for me. He and Tim would think up some plan between them. They would get Letroit out of the room. They would aid my escape. They *would* come for me!

But they didn't. No one came.

My phone quietly rumbled a few more times to inform me of incoming calls and, each time, I attempted to send a reply. But it was no use.

It was the longest, most torturous sixteen minutes of my life. The pain was unbearable. The stink was even worse. Desperate for something to take my mind off my situation, I rewrote my Personal Statement in my head.

JACK SAMSONITE'S PERSONAL STATEMENT: ATTEMPT #12

My name is Jack Samsonite.
I sniff balls.
Give me a scholarship.

My best attempt yet.

Then, finally, one of the greatest sounds known to man got one hundred times better – the end-of-school bell.

Letroit had sat there, in the empty room, obediently waiting for that bell to ring before he got to his feet and hobbled out through the doorway.

I didn't waste a second. The moment I heard that door click shut I clambered out from that fart-stinking nut-trap as fast as my numb, pins-and-needle-filled legs would permit. God knows where Letroit had gone, but he'd left his bag, jacket and trumpet behind. He was going to come back, but I didn't hang around to find out when that would be. I grabbed that stupid trumpet, checked the coast was clear then ran from that room as though it were Hell itself.

Unfortunately, it would appear that Hell is capable of running just as fast as me.

THE RACE IS ON

I tried calling James six more times whilst I searched the rapidly emptying school for him and Tim (at least I *think* I was ringing James. The only part of his name visible on my cracked and bleeding screen was '. . ame . ', but I was fairly certain he was the only '. . ame . ' in my address book). After ten minutes of fruitless searching, my phone finally began to vibrate. '. . ame . ' was calling me.

'Where are you?' James asked, sounding slightly put out.

'What?!'

'Where are you sitting?' he demanded.

'I'm not sitting anywhere! I'm looking for you!'

'Well, we're looking for you! Where are you?!'

'I'm on my way out of the common room for the third time in ten minutes. Where are you?'

'You're what? What the . . . ? We're at the pub!'

Disappointment, betrayal and fierce anger surged through my veins like a dizzying poison.

'What the hell are you doing at the pub?' I raged. 'I've been stuck here with my face in Letroit's ball-bag! I needed your help!'

'You *what*!' James raged back, with a hint of a laugh. 'Why did you tell me you were at the pub then, you twat?'

'I DIDN'T!'

'YES, YOU DID! Here . . . this is the last text you sent me, out of all your bollocked-up wank-texts . . . 3.55 p.m. – "INDER the dwaj"!'

I waited for him to say something that resembled English. He waited for me to reply.

'What?' I hissed.

'That's what you sent me! *Inder the dwaj!*'

'UNDER THE DESK!' I roared. 'I was under the cock-sniffing desk! I needed your help! And you went to the pub?'

'That's where you said you were!'

'How the hell does "inder the dwaj" mean I'm in the pub?'

'Well, how does it mean "under the desk"?'

'How could I even have got to the pub so fast? It's a twenty-minute walk!'

'I don't know! You got a lift?'

'With who? Superman? I sent you a text right after you left the media room!'

'Yeah!' agreed James. 'A text of frickin' bullshit!'

'Fine,' I relented. 'Whatever. I'll see you there.'

I was about ready to rip someone's head off. I had gone through all that crap – sniffed balls, retrieved the trumpet – and I didn't even get a 'well done' or 'thank you'! So you will understand why, after what James said next, I all but exploded with rage.

'Whatever, take your time. We can film without you, anyway . . .' He waited for a response that never came. 'We decided that, since you haven't exactly nailed the girl-getting thing, and since I'm kind of an established character in the film now, maybe I should have a crack at the kiss thing. You know, to like, maximise our chances of finishing this thing.'

I translated that to mean: 'We're taking over the film. It's mutiny. I'm going to be the star, and I'm going to get it on with one of your favourite girls, on camera. You're out of the loop. It's war.'

I couldn't let this happen. I had to get there as fast as I could. I had to talk to Em, to Edith, to Sally. I had to get my kiss. I wasn't going to let James take this from me. And if he did ... if he crowned himself hero of the film ... if he got it on with one of them ... then he would find he had the most determined enemy he could ever face.

'Who else is there?' I asked.

'Everyone,' he replied.

Crap.

I hung up the phone.

And I didn't even say goodbye.

THE VOICE

I hid the trumpet in the common room then left the school grounds with fierce determination in every powerful step. I could not get to that pub soon enough. My superhero status depended on it. No, screw my superhero status: my future in kissing girls depended on it.

Yes, that *is* very sad. My media studies grade, Personal Statement, university placement and career as a screen-writer may also have been somewhat dependent on it but, at that moment in time, I did not care about any of those things. My goal was more immediate, as would be the reward. I was going to snog a girl, and I wasn't about to let anyone or anything halt my progress. Except ...

I was really hungry. I mean *really* hungry, like my-stomach-is-eating-itself kind of hungry. At first I thought I could hold on, last out until I got to the pub then fill the hole with crisps and nuts, but after five minutes of power walking I realised I was going to have to get food or risk passing out on the way (I figured a two-minute pit-stop to refuel would be more beneficial than a face-dive into the pavement and a long, slow, malnourished crawl to the Dog and Gun).

But halfway through my mountain of heavy, stodgy, greasy chips (plus tub of mushy peas, which I did not order or want, yet ended up paying for anyway), my bottom suddenly informed me that large amounts of food may not actually supply the boost in speed that I required. In fact, if anything, it had slowed me down even more, as it forced me into a butt-clenching, poo-retaining waddle.

There were only two things I could do to speed up my journey:

1. **I could poo in a nearby hedge (which, surprisingly, seemed more appealing than finding a public toilet)**
2. **I could continue to hold it in, and take the short cut.**

As much as I do not like the shortcut (a canal-side footpath that's dark, scary and usually patrolled by a crazy old glue-sniffing mentalist), it won out over option one, by quite a long way.

As I approached the shortcut, I hoped that it would either be busy with nice, sensible, middle-aged dog-walkers, or completely empty. When it turned out to be completely empty I was slightly disappointed to not have the company of sensible dog-walkers, but it was better than it being over-flowing with criminals and arseholes.

It was also uncomfortably quiet, and I did my best to walk lightly, so as not to make too much noise on the gravelly path. Even though it wasn't due to get dark for another hour or two, the tall, overhanging trees of the neighbouring woodland, combined with an overcast sky, gave the impression of an early and perpetual dusk.

This was good. Not only did the shortcut reduce the distance of my journey, but also the crap-scariness of it forced me to walk more quickly than a normal person would. The further I progressed down the path, the greater my confidence became and, soon enough, I was back to walking at full speed and full volume, feeling silly for having been such a scaredy-cat.

And that's when I heard the voice.

Or, at least, I thought it was a voice. It was such a faint and short little whimper that I wasn't even sure I'd heard anything at all. Nevertheless, it caused my entire heart to stop beating and twelve per cent of it to simply explode with alarm. (I didn't show it on the outside, though. Yes, even in this situation, where I was potentially faced with meeting a face-slicing, formaldehyde-preserving, corpse-shagging nut-job, I was still worried about looking silly in front of any non-existent passing joggers who might snigger at me jumping at a little noise.)

I casually (yet somewhat jerkily) glanced over my shoulder, only to see nothing behind me whatsoever. This was no surprise. The noise had sounded as if it had come from the ground, on the other side of the wire-mesh fence that separated the path from the surrounding woodland.

It was nothing, I told myself.

No one is here.

You're not going to get hurt.

Of all those lies, it was that last one that I believed the most. And that was what scared me the most too, because, as

I continued to walk away from the source of the noise, some-thing in my head caused me to slow down, just a fraction.

What if someone else is hurt? What if some poor lady has been victim to some hideous sexual assault and is bleeding to death in a hedge?

It wasn't an altogether serious thought, but the instant I thought it, the potential possibility of it felt horribly real. The thought sent a trembling chill down my spine.

It was nothing. Don't be silly. Just keep walking!

But I could not shake the image from my head.

What if someone is genuinely dying back there, and that whimper was a desperate plea for my help?

The fear was beginning to make me feel sick.

What could I do to help, though?

No. Don't be an arsehole. That could be someone's mum back there.

Or someone's little sister.

Then I began to picture the news headlines the next morning. I imagined hearing that a girl had been badly beaten, and slowly bled to death overnight. How could I ever live with myself, knowing that I could have helped?

I stopped walking. I turned around, and I headed back to where I thought I had heard the voice.

I moved quietly. As calmly as possible. Trying to ignore the thundering fear that was causing my muscles to quiver and my lungs to shudder with every breath. I knew that I was probably going to find either nothing at all, or just some small hedge-dwelling creature, but then I saw a torch proba-bly about one hundred yards away, searching in the darkness of the woods.

This is not normal.

Something was definitely wrong. The only reasons I could possibly think of that someone would be searching the woods in this light were: a) someone was investigating a suspicious disturbance, or maybe even a phone call to the emergency services, b) someone had lost a dog, or c) someone was searching for their victim, to finish the job off.

Shit!

I hunkered down slightly, in case it was option c). I stared through the fence to the point where I had heard the noise.

I crept closer. I saw nothing. Leaves. Twigs. Darkness. Nothing.

Thank god!

I was just about to turn back. And then ...

FUH ...

THE FACE

Pure terror exploded inside me.

Every major organ in my body collapsed. A jolt of shock brought them back, kicking and screaming, as my brain relayed what my eyes were seeing.

A hand.

A white, motionless hand.

Fingers clutching the wire mesh.

Desperate, yet unmoving.

And beyond that hand ...

A face!

Pale and still.

Bathed in shadow.

Eyes.

Glistening.

Motionless.

Open.

Staring straight up at me.

WARM, MUSHY AND
TRICKLING DOWN MY LEG

The body was completely motionless. It rested on the
ground in front of me – crouched, coiled and cowering. And
then it blinked. That miniscule, silent movement sent a bolt
of terror shooting through my body. It was like being kicked
in the chest by a horse.

JESUS CHRIST!

The fear was so intense it actually hurt.

There was no more movement, but there was a sound, a
rustle, then something else caught my eyes. A foot. It was at
an unnatural angle, backwards to how it should have been.

Is the leg completely snapped? Oh Jesus ...

But then the foot moved, and another stab of fear immo-
bilised me as I realised that the foot was attached to another
person, resting against a fallen tree, also staring at me. And
beside that face was *another*!

It suddenly became very clear that these three young lads
were definitely not victims of an assault.

And if they're not the victims, then they must be the ...

'Fuck off!' whispered the first sitting face, coarsely.

This quiet outburst shocked an unconscious backwards step out of me.

'We're playing hide and fucking seek!' the second sitting face spat, angrily.

'Sorry,' I muttered, quickly turning to walk away.

Hide and seek? Hide and frickin' seek? *I had courageously risked life and limb to make sure that the owner of that voice was not in need of help, and they tell me to fuck off because they're playing HIDE AND SEEK! And I said 'SORRY'?!*

The mixture of fear and anger boiled inside me like a toxic brew, and, without even thinking, I called out to the searching torch.

'They're over here!'

And the onslaught began.

'You FUCKING twat!' one roared.

'Ruin our fucking game, why don't you?'

'You total prick!'

I continued to walk and they began to follow me on the other side of the wire-mesh fence. They moved in and out of shadows so it was hard to be sure, but these guys looked kind of small, even as young as eleven or twelve, maybe? I didn't stop to stare.

'What the fuck?' called a voice from behind the torch, marching towards us.

'What d'ya do that for?' demanded the first sitting face, marching alongside me. 'You fucking prick!'

'I thought you were hurt!' I offered, with a pathetic, half-hearted shout.

'Who is this prick?' called the approaching torch-voice.

243

By this point it was apparent that there was not just one torch-voice, there were at least three.

'Some wanker who thinks it's fun to fuck up other people's games!' called the first sitting face.

And then he spat at me. The main bulk of the flob missed my face but the spray caught my neck. Burning with fury, I ignored it, wiped my neck with my sleeve, and carried on marching down the dark path.

There were now six of them in pursuit. The fact that we were separated by an eight-foot fence didn't quell my fears.

And then came another spit. Then another, and another. Three of them were marching alongside me and continually launching phlegm at my face.

'Piss off!' I complained, feebly trying to protect my head with my arm.

One of them must have found a handful of gravel from somewhere because the next thing I knew, a surprisingly painful bombardment of stones smashed against my skull.

'Jesus!' I gasped. And, as my mouth opened, a large slug of dickhead phlegm splatted across my bottom lip.

And then I snapped.

In an explosion of rage, I span and (for some reason) roared, like a puny little pink Incredible Hulk. I lashed out. I kicked the fence. I threw handfuls of leaves. And then I did something really silly. In retaliation for their spit-shower, I hurled my tub of mushy peas at them.

Now, as everyone knows, the correct procedure in mushy-pea deployment is to firstly remove the lid; then, keeping hold of the tub, launch the contents at your desired target. I, being a mushy-pea-fighting novice, did none of this. I

244

simply hurled that tub with all my might, lid and all. The tub hit the wire fence side-on and face-up. The lid pinged off and the contents spewed upwards, before raining copiously down. It appeared that it was me and the first sitting face that got the majority of the fallout. I was completely covered. Patches of clothing clung to my skin as warm, green mush trickled down me. My green-faced pursuer came to a halt, gave a knowing and angry smirk, took a step forward, out of the shadows, then slowly shook his head. His sudden wide eyes revealed that, at the exact time that I recognised who *he* was, he also recognised who *I* was.

'Gay boy!' Tyler growled. 'You did not want to do that.'

Then, much to my horror, he bent down, pulled up a loose piece of fence, and began to crawl through to my side. In my moment of horrified panic, I pushed him back through the fence, using my foot, in his face, really hard, and very fast.

And that was the second time in one day that I made little eleven-year-old Tyler (the Pygmy Warrior General) cry.

CRYLER

I watched in horror at what I'd done. Tyler clutched at his flattened, reddened face, howling the most ungodly noise I have ever heard. I then noticed that his entire gang of Year 7 friends had all scootched under the fence and were coming at me, full force.

I yelped. I turned. I ran. Very, very fast.

They too ran. Very faster.

Luckily, I had a trick up my sleeve.

And if you replace the word 'trick' with 'trip' and the words 'up my sleeve' with 'down a steep drop', you will get a good idea of my genius. Yes, they were faster than me, but they weren't as brave. Just as I was about to be taken down, my foot came up against something large and trippy.

After I had bounced off a few trees, slid through a thicket of bracken, plunged through a gaping hole in a fence, and emerged at a roadside, I knew that they wouldn't be brave enough to follow me down the almost sheer drop that I had just courageously fallen down.

It was over. No harm done. Apart from a few major blows to the head, some cuts and bruises, a couple of knocks to the head, torn clothes, a failing heart, trembling hands, one or two cracks to the head, wobbly legs, being covered in mushy peas and not really knowing where or who I was any more, it was as if it had never happened.

Everything was cool.

MY NAME IS JACKMAN
AND I AM SUPER-COOL

I staggered into the Dog and Gun. Everyone was having a good time. The noise was dauntingly loud. I hobbled weakly towards the back of the pub, where I could see familiar faces from school. At first I went completely unnoticed. But slowly, one by one, people began to spot me – a trembling wreck. Clothes torn. Lungs heaving desperately for oxygen. Face scratched. Covered in dry leaves. Splattered in all kinds of mess.

'Jack?' gasped Em, rushing to my aid. 'What happened?'

I just stood there, not quite able to form proper words, numb with shock, whilst Em tried to coax some kind of explanation from me.

'Jack! Talk to me!' she ordered in a worried panic, whilst a swarm of curious onlookers drifted closer.

Unfortunately, I had completely forgotten about the whole *JackMan, super-cool, star of a film* thing, and somehow, something resembling the truth dribbled from my mushy-pea mouth.

'Some kids were playing hide and seek, but I thought they

had been raped, so I threw mushy peas at them and kicked one in the face,' I said to Em.

I don't think I came across quite as heroically as I'd originally intended. Then, after my heartfelt and eloquent speech, drunk on my new-found respect for life, I went and ruined it by saying something silly.

'Em . . .' I murbled, snapping out of my zombie-like state just enough to look her in the eyes, 'I need to lose my virginity with my mouth.'

And then, I can't be certain, but it's possible I may have cried a tiny bit.

THIS IS NOT THE END

As far as I was concerned, I had just suffered a horrific, near-death experience; I had reached my destination, reached the end of my story, and was feeling highly emotional and kind of *carpe diem*-ish, and that's why I had just come straight out and told Em I wanted to kiss her (in a roundabout way). But, as far as Em was concerned, I was a wobbly twat with mushy peas all over himself, deliriously confessing his desire to have mouth-sex, in a dingy old pub. Not as romantic as it felt from my point of view.

'OK, I think we need to get you out of here,' Em said, with an authoritative tone.

I think I just humiliated myself.

'Jack?' said Em, attempting to make some kind of connection.

'Yes,' I replied, calmly.

'Come on, outside,' she shooed.

Go somewhere alone with Em? That sounds good.

Well, the words sounded good – outside with Em – but the way she was saying them was not (like I was a naughty child).

'Am I naughty?' I asked.

I think that sounded weird.

'Jack?' she said slowly and clearly. 'Are you drunk?'

'No, I ... I got punched in the head a couple of times, I think.'

(Please do not panic, I have not been so unjust as to tell you an untruth about my escape. I did not get punched one single time. I was merely lying. In actual fact, I had head-butted a few trees and face-planted the ground a couple of times, but I was regaining enough sense to know that those pieces of truth would not assist my attempts at appearing heroic.)

'Right. Outside. Now,' she ordered.

Yes!

'No!'

There might be kids with peas out there!

Aha! I didn't say that out loud! Things are getting better!

'Jack ...' she said, warningly.

'I don't like mushy peas,' I whined.

Or ... maybe not.

'Jack, I really think we should go outside.' Em nodded emphatically.

'Did I just make a tit of myself?' I asked, feeling slightly less dazed now.

'No, it's fine, just ... let's go out of here at least,' she suggested.

'What's wrong?' I demanded. 'I think I'm OK!'

The increasing numbers of people gathering around was making an increasing amount of noise, and I wasn't sure if some of those noises were titters and giggles, which was making me increasingly uneasy.

'Are they ... *laughing* at me?' I asked, in disgust.

Is Sean Palmer laughing at me? I just ...

'You got something you want to say, Sharmer?' I asked, angrily.

Sean smirked, shook his head and held a hand up, trying not to burst into a fit of giggles.

'I just got attacked by six people!' I yelled. 'You think that's funny, do you?'

Clearly my anger from the incident had not entirely subsided.

Em spun round and shot the swarm of people a killer, disapproving glare.

'Just ignore them, Jack. Most of them are drunk.'

'No! I ... '

'Jack!' she warned.

'What?' I demanded.

'Outside! Please!'

'No! I think I actually just want to ... '

'Jack!' she barked again.

'What?' I barked back.

'Your penis is hanging out! OK?'

HANGING OUTSIDE

Em was right. I think going outside was definitely a good idea. But as we sat in the bus stop across the road, no amount of Em's reassurances was ever going to stop this from being the worst thing to ever happen to me. She spoke to my face for ... I don't know how long, but it was a long time before my brain re-engaged and I actually heard what she was saying.

'I'm fine,' my mouth lied to her, whilst my mind continued its torrent of expletives.

'Come on, then,' she tried to coerce me. 'Let's go back inside and pretend it never happened.'

'Ha!' my mouth laughed, whilst my brain screamed, *I don't think so!*

'Well, I'm going back in because I'm freezing, and I'm not leaving you out here on your own,' she said sternly.

'I'm fine. Honestly. I just want to be by myself for a while. I'll just go for a walk and see you later.'

'I'm really not ... ' she tried again.

'It's OK! I'm a big boy!'

In light of my recent exposure, I think she knew that to be a great, big, shrivelled, little lie.

'I can't believe my nob was out,' I groaned, hanging my head in my hands.

'Will you stop going over this?' she pleaded. 'I told you, it wasn't completely out – you couldn't even see the end!'

'That doesn't mean *anything*!' I insisted.

'Yes! It does!' she growled, getting tired of reassuring me.

'You saw my nob,' I sighed. 'That's all it boils down to. Everyone saw my nob. It doesn't matter how much of it they saw. Nob is nob!'

There was no denying such grounded philosophy – nob certainly is nob.

'Fine,' Em said with a note of finality as she straightened herself up. 'Look.'

And then she pulled her top down.

And then. She pulled. Her top ... *down*!

No, you didn't read it wrong. Just to clarify – SHE PULLED HER TOP DOWN.

In actual fact, she tugged on one side of the neckline of her blousy hippy thing (I don't know the names of all these different types of girl-clothing), until her right boob was all but hanging out.

Ho-ly shiiiiit!

I could not believe what was happening! One minute I was as low as I could possibly get; the next minute I was in danger of blowing the top off my head! It was like I'd just found out my cat was dead, so someone zapped me with one of those electric heart-starter paddle things!

This was *way* more consolation than I had expected!

'There! If you can't see a nipple, does it count as seeing a boob?' she asked, with tired anger.

Ho-ly shiiiiiiiiiiiiiiiit!

'I *can* see your nipple.'

She looked down.

'Shit!' she gasped, realising she'd pulled her top down further than she'd intended.

Yes, just peeking out over the tops of her knuckles had been a beautiful pink splodge – the single piece of treasure I had spent my life searching for – my white whale, my Holy Grail . . .

It took me a moment to absorb what exactly had just happened.

I just saw my first ever bare-naked boob!

A nipple!

A REAL-LIFE NIPPLE!

(Well, half of one, but that still counts right?) I was speechless.

A BOOB!!!

Covered in peas, in a deserted bus stop at the dodgy end of town was not quite how I had imagined my first ever nippling, but I wasn't complaining.

Em was mortified.

'I can't believe I just did that!' she whispered to herself, being a lot more bashful about it than I ever would have expected.

I took it upon myself to give her some reassurance, as she had just done for me and my bare-naked willy.

Go on, say something to make her feel better.

'I just saw your boob,' was unfortunately all my mushy little brain could cook up right then.

'Thanks, Jack,' she groaned. 'I'm aware of that.'

I said, '*SAY SOMETHING TO MAKE HER FEEL BETTER*'!

'Well . . . '

Come on, Jack, she is struggling and you're a superhero.
You can fix this.

'Erm . . . '

Use the force . . .

'It was a nice shape!'

'Jack!' she moaned, disapprovingly.

No? Well . . . I don't think I have anything else!

'I only saw one!' I chirped optimistically. 'It doesn't count
if you only see one!'

Oh, I'm a lying genius!

'Nice try,' she grunted.

Or not.

'I think I'll go now,' she whispered, pointing back to the
pub.

'OK,' I mimic-whispered, pointing in the opposite direction. 'Me, too. See you in a bit.'

And so we went off in our separate directions.

Em saw my willy and I saw her boob . . . man, I'm almost
not a virgin any more!

IT'S SO ON

'Are you ever coming to the pub or what?' asked the female voice inside my phone.

What the hell?

First of all, how could anyone not know that I hadn't not been to the pub already? (I'm sure there must be a way of saying that without it hurting my head). And, second of all …

Who the hell am I talking to?

The only information my cracked phone would divulge about the caller's identity was an 'i', and that could really have just been the 'i' from the words 'incoming call'.

I did not have a clue how to reply to this.

'Wherr?' I asked. (See?)

'Where are you?' the voice asked.

Is that Sally Kirk?

'Errr … kind of halfway,' I lied.

'You may as well head straight for my place then,' the voice said chirpily.

Edith?

'It's kind of dead here, anyway,' she yelled over the raucous noise in the background.

257

'Doesn't sound very dead,' I contradicted, like an idiot.

'Oh, that's just everyone getting over-excited about some weirdo showing Sean Palmer his penis,' she explained.

Is she mocking me, or does she genuinely not know?

'Oh,' I replied.

'It would have been a lot better if you'd been here, though,' she said, in a complainy sort of way.

A warm glow began to radiate from my chest. I'm not usually very good at spotting when a girl is coming on to me, but this left me in no doubt. I couldn't hold back the huge smile that invaded my face.

'Why?' I probed, keen to hear more.

'Because you've still got my bag, you big idiot!' she giggle-shouted. 'I put it in your bag and now I can't buy any drinks!'

The warm glow suddenly transformed into tepid arse-juice. The smile died.

Oh.

'Oh.'

Shit.

'Shit.'

I want to cry again.

'Sorry.'

'Don't worry about it.' Her voice smiled. 'Just let yourself into my house. My dad won't be home for hours and there's some pizzas you could stick in the oven, if you wouldn't mind?'

My heart began to lift again, if only by a fraction.

She's deserting the lively pub in favour of me? We're going to spend the evening together and have pizza?

OK, this was getting better. Admittedly, I was still feeling a kind of pang for Em and her boob, but I pushed it out of my mind. She was probably back in the pub, wrapped up in Charlie's arms, preparing for a night of horrible sex.

'Sure,' I agreed happily.

'Awesome, babes. There's a spare key somewhere in my bag. You know where it is, right?'

'Your bag?'

'My house. I live next door to Tim, OK?'

'Oh, yeah, I know.'

Lucky bastard!

'OK, catch you in a bit, hun!'

And she was gone.

And I began to run. If I was quick, then I might have time to clean some of the dog crap and mushy peas off my trousers before she got back. Or, even better . . .

I might even be able to poo!

EDITH'S HOUSE

I didn't get there as fast as I'd have liked due to the fact that the mushy peas had soaked right through my jeans and had then begun to dry, which meant that every time I took a step, the pea-glue-trouser combo was ripping hairs from my thighs.

When I finally did get to Edith's house, I realised I was not alone.

If only I'd carried on walking! They would have realised no one was home, then left!

But I'm never that clever in the heat of the moment.

'Hi!' I said politely, as Edith's grandparents crossed the front garden. 'I'm Jack, a friend of Edith's.'

'Oh, hello, dear!' the little old lady said, cheerfully.

Edith's grandad didn't say anything, but gave me the warmest, most enthusiastic smile I've ever seen.

'Edith's on her way,' I explained. 'She sent me ahead to get the food on.'

'Oh, lovely!' the smiley little wrinkle-faced lady enthused.

Oh Jesus, did she take that as an invite to join us? They're going to stay all evening, aren't they?

'We're not stopping for long though,' I quickly added, thinking fast, 'because we're going to the cinema.'

'Oh, lovely! Did you hear that?' she asked, turning to her smiley husband.

'Ye-as,' he nodded, kind of gormlessly.

'Edith's got a new boyfriend and he's taking her to the pictures!' she shouted at him.

'Ye-as,' he responded, still gormlessly.

'And where do you ...?' she began asking me, before being interrupted by her happy little husband.

'I know, I heard,' he replied, thirty seconds too late.

'Oh, give over!' she muttered. 'Come on. Let's not catch a chill.'

That comment was aimed at her husband, but I got the impression it was a hint for me to let them in. I held the door open, let them both gormlessly wobble inside, hoping they might get a whiff of my pea and poo pants, and then make a sharp exit. Unfortunately, it would appear that they were at that age where elderly people lose the ability to detect pea and poo.

Edith's home wasn't as hippy-ish as I had pictured it. It was actually surprisingly bland, characterless and 100 per cent Ikea. The fact that it was so generic worked in my favour, though, as it made it extremely simple to navigate. The freezer was exactly where it seemed it should have been. I rummaged through it, but only found one pizza.

Edith said pizzas, *right? Plural.*

I used my initiative and pulled out a substitute lasagne.

Balls! Do I offer the grandparents food, too?

I knew that if we wanted to get rid of them soon then I

was going to have to ignore them, but my politeness won through in the end.

I can't make dinner right in front of them and not even offer them anything!

I always feel like such a fake when I'm around old people, acting so nice and mature that I make even myself feel sick.

'Would you like something to eat?' I offered.

'Oh, look at this!' the old lady beamed. 'Hasn't she got him trained well?'

It did occur to me to correct her about the whole boyfriend thing, but I just couldn't be bothered. You know what old people are like. They probably wouldn't get it (plus I kind of liked it).

'Don't you worry about us, dear – you go on and see to yourself,' she smiled.

The way she said it definitely made it sound like they intended to stay.

Please, no! I'm supposed to be having a sleepover! With a girl! We might play Spin the Bottle, which might lead to Naked Twister, which might lead to Hide the Willy in the Woo-woo! It just won't be any fun if a bunch of old people try to join in!

I'm guessing their senses must *really* have been on their last legs because, now that I was in an enclosed space and out of the fresh air, the horrible stench of re-hydrated dog poo and peas was becoming overpowering. Yet they didn't bat an eyelid.

I have to do something about this before Edith gets back.

Once the food was in the oven, I excused myself and

headed to the bathroom, making sure to take my bag with me.

'Right!' I said to myself, as I whipped my crusty clothes off and searched through my bag for BO emergency spares. 'Sort yourself out.'

Knowing that time was short before Edith would return home, I moved with superhuman speed. I threw my stupid trousers into the bath, switched the shower attachment on full blast, and gave them a quick jet-wash. Yes, they were going to be soaking, but wetness trumps eye-watering poo-pea-stink every time. I wrung them out as best I could, then pulled the blind up, opened the window, hung my trousers out of it (it was a back window, so Edith wouldn't see them on approach). The worst of the mushy peas had completely gone, but the dog-poo stains were apparently here to stay. As long as the smell had gone, that was the main thing.

I then grabbed my emergency T-shirt and deodorant from my bag (I get sweaty – it's a hormone thing apparently). I draped my pea-damp boxers over the shower rail in preparation to rinse myself down at the sink but, before I had turned the taps on, I heard my phone ringing from my trouser pocket, outside the window.

Crap!

Thanks to its recent bath, the screen now showed no name at all, but I knew it was likely to be James, Em or Edith.

'Jack?' said the voice.

'Sally?' I said, trying my hardest to not sound like a naked person.

'What. The. *Fuck*. Is. Going. On?' she asked, sounding kind of intense.

Oh, dear. What now?

'Why,' she asked, 'are you NAKED?'

ORANGE ORANGE PENIS SNAKE!

I instantly began to panic.

How the hell does she know I'm naked?

And then I saw ... the answer was right in front of me. There, outside the window, just a few back-gardens away, was Sally, and about a dozen other people, all looking straight at me.

NOOOOOOOO!!!!!!!

I instantly dropped to the floor in a confused and violated frenzy.

'What the hell are you doing?' I squealed.

'We're having a party! What are *you* doing?'

They're having a what?

'I'm at Edith's!' I explained, angry at the invasion of my privacy.

'No, Jack. *We're* at Edith's. You're in Mr and Mrs Flower's bathroom!'

I'm what?

I'm ...

In who ...?

What?

I'm ...
Oh.
Dear.
God.
'Dinner's ready, dear!'

MAKING A MEAL OF IT

I swear to god, if it hadn't been a concrete patio below, I would have jumped, there and then. As it was, I had to go back downstairs and face them.

These people are not Edith's grandparents.

This is not Edith's house.

These people are Tim's neighbours – on the <u>other</u> side!

These people are absolutely insane . . .

As I slowly put my pea-pants and dripping-wet trousers back on, I realised it must have only been the Flowers' kitchen that had been Ikea-pimped. How did I miss all the signs? The lace doily underneath the plant pots, the frilly cover around the toilet brush holder, the fact that the front door was already open when I got there . . . It was like that revelation bit at the end of *The Sixth Sense*, only much, much worse, especially as, when I opened the bathroom door . . .

The smell!

Oh god, that smell! It hadn't been my shitty-pea pants after all. It was *them*!

I smell old people! Poo-and-wee stinking, crazy old people!

'I'll put Edith's plate in the oven to keep warm until she arrives,' Old Wrinkly-face smiled as I cautiously entered the kitchen.

There it was. All laid out on the table. One pizza and one lasagne, on two plates, with accompanying side salad and two glasses of lumpy milk.

I have to get out of here!

But how? What is the usual protocol in this type of situation? I invited myself into their house and made myself dinner with their food! Can I really just run? But, also, I couldn't seriously do the polite thing and stay to eat, could I?

'Do the strange thing!' I heard Pumpkin's advice echo through my head.

Shut the hell up, Pumpkin! The only way this could get any stranger would be for me to rub that pizza into my genitals then dance the hula with a lampshade on my head!

'This looks LUUUVly!' I enthused.

What the crapping hell am I going to do?

It was no use. No matter how long I stood there, staring at the plates of food, and asking myself what to do, my brain was refusing to respond. My well of amazing ideas was all dried up and all that remained at the bottom was an old boot and a dead mouse.

So, I did the only thing my conscience would allow. I sat down and started eating, whilst Old Smiley Wrinkles stood beside me and watched.

This is the freakiest thing I have ever done.

The thought of forcing more food into my bowels made my insides begin to tremble.

I'm not even hungry!

There was a very real danger that just one mouthful of lasagne was going to be the last thing I ever ate.

Something inside me might explode! Or, even worse, I've heard that if you go too long without pooing, your body finds the only other way of getting it out of you ... it brings it back up through your mouth!

Can you imagine that? As if puking isn't horrible enough! But puking *poo*? However, if I was going to do the polite thing, then eat that food I must. If I vomited diarrhoea all over their nice white tablecloth as a consequence, then so be it. At least they couldn't accuse me of being rude.

Don't think about it. Just eat it, then get out of here!

I shovelled that food down me so unbelievably fast that I barely even chewed. It wasn't easy. Especially when you're being watched. And it was made even harder when I glanced over to the window and ...

'Arghh!' I yelled, startled half to death by the sight of James, Tim and a video camera staring in at me.

I turned to see if my outburst had alerted the old lady to their presence, but she simply continued to smile and stare.

She's so frickin' old that she didn't even notice me scream in her FACE!

If it hadn't been for her eyeballs flitting between my plate and my face, I'd have sworn she had died standing up.

James gave a huge quizzical shrug and mouthed the word, 'Waddafugyadoon?!' (At least, that's what it looked like he was saying.) I gave only the subtlest of grimace-shrugs – *help!* James made a gesture that I missed and then he dropped out of sight. Seconds later, my phone began to ring.

'Oop! That's me,' I said, pulling my phone from my pocket.

'Oh, that's nice!' she complimented, thinking I was producing my phone simply to show it to her.

'It's Edith,' I explied, loudly and clearly.

'Oh, it's Edith's?'

'No. It's Edith *calling* me.'

'Oh, is she? Where?' she asked, finally breaking from her frozen pose and heading for the door. 'Outside?'

'NO,' I yelled. 'Edith – is – calling – me – on – the – *phone*!'

'Oh!' she gasped, picking up the receiver of her giant beige telephone from 1962. 'Hello?'

Oh, my holy god!

'Hello?' I said to James, as I answered my phone.

'Is that Edith?' the old lady said into her phone.

'You absolute frickin' idiot!' James roared with laughter.

'Are you going to do her?' I heard Tim giggle excitedly.

'Are you going to lick her wrinkly nipples?' James added.

'Yeah, sure. OK, bye. Bye!' I hung up the phone then.

I stabbed my fork into a solid lump of frozen lasagne, then decided I couldn't take any more. Whilst the old lady continued her conversation with a dialling tone, I got out of my seat and made a break for the front door.

Her hand reached out and stopped me.

'It's Edith!' she whispered, pointing to the receiver and passing it to me.

Keep going! I told myself, *Do not stop! Her husband will appear from a cupboard and club you to death with a dead dog!*

Ignoring my fears, I nervously took the phone from her. 'Hello?' I said.

The dialling tone purred in my ear.

'Oh my god!' I hollered. 'OK, bye!'

I hung up the phone and dashed to the door.

'It's Edith!' I explained, mid escape. 'She's ... stuck ... somewhere. And there's a dead dog! I have to go!'

And so I went, as fast as my wet little legs would carry me, away from what will for ever be the weirdest experience of my entire life.

LET THE PARTY START

The sprint into Edith's back garden was way too short. I didn't want to stop that soon. I just wanted to run and run and keep going until I was as far away from that place as possible. Two doors down the road was not an adequate escape. But at least there would be no old people. There would be no foul stench. There would be Edith. And there would be ...

Laughter. Lots and lots of laughter, plus a huge round of applause greeted me as I stumbled into Edith's post-pub party.

I should have known it was too good to be true. Edith must have finally decided that she didn't want to be alone with me after all, so had invited the whole pub back for protection. Or was this the plan all along? Was it always going to be a party? Was I invited to a group sleepover?

Either way, I had been served a large helping of rejection and total failure, with a side-order of public humiliation and a dollop of ridicule. Disappointment draped itself around me like a big, wet, stinky blanket as I trudged numbly past all the laughing faces and derisive comments.

'Jack, mate, your penis is all over Facebook!' laughed Iain

Vinleigh as he came rushing over to thrust his mobile phone in my face.

I was still too shell-shocked to process just how bad that was as I glanced at the blurred and pixelated picture of me standing in a pub with something pink in my zipper.

'You can't even see the end,' I muttered dismissively as I carried on walking, trying to ignore the non-stop jokes at my expense.

'Jack got lucky already!'

'Way to go! She was hot!'

'Getting it on with a G-G-G-GILF!'

'What the hell's a G-G-G-GILF?' asked Sally.

'A great great great grandma I'd like to f—'

'OK, I get it.'

Finally, a friendly face approached.

'Dude!' laughed James, camera still rolling. 'We must be able to use some of this! It's gold!'

If he means we're going to use footage of me, exposing myself in an old-people's house, for our film, then he is sorely mistaken.

'I don't think so,' I muttered.

'Can you take the camera?' he asked.

'No, James,' I murbled. 'I'm really not in the mood right now.'

'Well, when you're in the mood? Soon? Because . . . ' – he glanced back to a circle of people sitting on the grass, where the only face that I recognised was Em – then, with wide-eyed excitement, concluded, 'I'm *so* getting it on later!'

I was half-tempted to punch him in the face there and then.

Stay away from my Em!

But common sense reminded me that one of those other unfamiliar faces, sitting over in that group, was probably the famous Charlie. Plus, there were a dozen girls James could have been referring to.

'There's something I kind of need to talk to you about,' James began. 'I think you . . . '

'Jack!' Tim called, running over to us. 'I've done it! I've fixed the problem!'

'What problem?' I asked.

'I found someone for you to kiss!' he panted, high-fiving the air where my hand wasn't, accidentally hitting my ear.

'Who?' asked James.

'Her!' beamed Tim, pointing to a girl at the other end of the garden.

'Tim, she looks about twelve,' James informed him.

'I know, but she's totally up for it! And, get this . . . ' Tim began frantically searching for a face in the crowd, before stopping to point at a huge, hairy beast of a man, '*that's* her brother! And he totally wants to smash your face in!'

Tim waited for another high five that never came.

'Why does he want to smash my face in, Tim?' I nervously muttered.

'Because you want to kiss his twelve-year-old sister!' Tim grinned proudly.

'You *told* him this?'

'Uh-huh!'

'You absolute, shitting idiot!'

'What?' Tim complained, as I began to sheepishly move towards the house and away from the huge, hairy beast-man.

274

'It's the perfect solution! Why am I the only one thinking logically here?'

'I'll try to fix it!' James called after me, as I made my hasty retreat.

I seriously hope he does.

'Two exposures in one evening? Nice work, honey.' Sally congratulated me as she joined me on my rapid walk of shame across the back garden and towards the house (making sure to keep my back to the beast-man). Then, when I didn't respond, she tugged at my arm, 'Come onnnnn! You've got to see the funny side!'

'There is no funny side,' I moaned, unable to hide my sick feeling from her.

'Oh, Jack, seriously, it's *nothing*!' she growled, with such sincerity that I actually began to believe her. 'It's such a *teeny weeny* little thing!'

My expression of utter dismay at what she had just said must have made her think twice about her choice of words.

'I mean the photo!' she hastily added. 'The *problem* is small. In a few weeks it'll be old news. Plus, it's not even a clear picture.'

'You can see my penis in it,' I reminded her.

'Barely!' she reasoned. 'It was only the top inch or two.'

Actually, there's no such thing as the top inch or two – that's pretty much the whole thing. But I wasn't about to make that public news.

'It doesn't even count if you don't see the *end*!' she added.

Is this some kind of rule that girls made up hundreds of years ago? Is this actually a thing, or is she just saying it to make me feel better?

275

'Plus, it's nothing we didn't all see in the bathroom window, anyway,' Sally muttered, with a teasing giggle.

'Please don't,' I groaned, not needing to be reminded.

'Oh, relax,' she sighed with a note of finality, and linked her arm tightly into mine.

Finally! Someone did something to make me feel better. She was being affectionate! Maybe this would help convince the beast-man that I wasn't interested in his little sister. Plus, Sally had seen my penis, twice, yet was still prepared to make physical contact with me. She wasn't repulsed. She wasn't treating me like a sicko. And she called me 'honey'!

Do I still actually stand a chance of scoring tonight? Or am I reading a bit too much into this?

'Anyway,' she added, going back to my problem. 'It's Sean Palmer who should be embarrassed, for taking the photo of it.'

'Yeah, great, thanks,' I said, finally managing a slight smile.

And, just as I was beginning to feel almost normal again, that's when I decided to walk backwards.

'What . . . are you doing?' Sally asked, as if it was a weird thing to do.

What I was doing was making sure that Gobby Cow from the bus, the one who threatened to have me beaten up for making Tyler cry, and who was standing right outside the back door to Edith's house, did not see me. What I was also doing was accidentally exposing my face in the direction of the hairy beast, so that he *could* see me (but he didn't). One quick change of plan later and I was walking *sideways* in through that back door (I'm quick on my feet like that).

'He'll definitely be here somewhere,' I heard her gobby voice speak into her gobby phone.

Is she talking about ME? Does everyone at this party want to hurt me? I really need to reduce my number of villains!

But then, as I stepped into Edith's kitchen, something genuinely amazing happened.

TOO GOOD TO BE TRUE

'There you are!' whooped Edith, spotting me from the other end of the room and rushing over to greet me with a big squeeze. 'Where have you *been*?'

Seriously? I've flashed my nob in public twice in one hour and you are still completely oblivious to it?

'Err ...' I stalled, wondering which version of the truth to tell her, 'Just ... hanging out.'

'He was looking after Mr and Mrs Flowers and it was *so* sweet,' Sally informed her.

'Are you being serious?' Edith asked. 'Doing what?'

'Oh, I ... made them lasagne and pizza and stuff,' I shrugged.

'And sausage!' Sally snorted, much to Edith's bewilderment.

'Well, now you're going to hang out with me because there's something that I need to tell you.'

'I don't think so!' Sally playfully warned her, still clinging tightly to my arm. 'He's mine!'

Is this seriously happening? Am I genuinely in demand, or are they messing with me? Does everyone at this party want to kiss me?

'Fight you for him!' Edith fake-scowled, clinging to my other arm.

I LIKE THIS! I LIKE THIS!

Sally scowled back, then finally relinquished me.

'Fine, take him,' she sang out, throwing her hands in the air. 'I've seen enough of him for one evening, anyway.'

'Yay!' Edith cheered, throwing her arms around me and claiming me as her own.

'But I want him back by eleven!' Sally warned.

'Oh, absolutely!' Edith assured her, with over-the-top, frowny sincerity.

'And don't wear him out too much!' Sally called, as Edith began to lead me away.

'Wouldn't dream of it!' Edith called back, without pausing.

'Right you,' she said authoritatively. 'You're coming to my room.'

My heart began to flip out, she put my hand in hers, and she took me upstairs.

BED

Upstairs is good. Upstairs is my friend. Upstairs is away from the people who want to hurt me, and closer to those who want to kiss my mouth with their mouth. Possibly.

'Sit down!' Edith invited, patting the large expanse of bed beside her.

Crikey! But how close do I sit? She's probably just being friendly, right? If I sit too close it could freak her out and send her running. But she might not just be being nice! She might want to kiss my mouth! And if I sit too far away she might think I don't think that she's pretty and adorable and totally kiss-on-the-mouth-able!

I decided that one thigh's-width apart would be just right. So I sat. On her hand! And, for the first time in my life, I made a girl squeal in the bedroom.

'Sorry!' I gasped, jumping back to my feet.

'Calm down,' she giggled, pulling me back onto the bed. 'You're not *that* heavy!'

The second my bum hit that mattress I became the most nervous and uncomfortable person on the planet.

Now what? What do I do with my hands? Do I face my

body towards her? Do I look into her eyes? Why don't these things come naturally to me?

'I thought you were such a dick the first time I met you,' she giggled, with an uncharacteristic level of embarrassment.

Oh. That's ... nice.

'But you're actually really sweet,' she said, turning to gaze into my eyes, 'despite what you say about my family.'

Oh my god. This is it! It's going to happen! I can feel it!

'When I saw you with your cousin ...' she trailed off, breaking eye contact to stare at her hands.

Oh, dear. I feel kind of bad now. Her entire image of me is based on lies. I've tricked a girl into bed! I've manipulated her in the worst way possible! Can I do this? How can I have sunk so low? I've tricked her into thinking I'm someone that I'm not. I'm no better than Superman!

'So, Jack ...' she purred slowly.

This made me very nervous!

'I was wondering ...' she continued.

A massage? A test to see if you're a good kisser or not? You want me to check to see if your nipples are aligned correctly? Anything!

'How would you like ...'

KNOCK! KNOCK! KNOCK!

NO, NO, NO!

The door swung open and Tim's stupid face poked inside.

'Hi I need to talk to Jack,' he blurted with zero punctuation, minimum politeness, maximum speed and extreme panic.

'I'll talk to you later, Tim,' I told him sternly. 'I'm just *talking to Edith* right now.'

Edith's phone then selfishly chose that exact moment to start ringing.

'It's fine,' she assured me, hopping off the bed and heading out of the room. 'You two talk. I need to take this.'

And then she was gone, striding across the landing and talking into her phone. 'Hi, Daaad!'

'You fucking twat!' I whisper-shouted at Tim, as he dashed into the room and closed the door behind him. 'Just because *you* can't have her doesn't mean you can sabotage my ...'

But I stopped short when I saw the look of sheer terror on his face, and knew in an instant that, somehow, for some reason, we were in serious trouble.

'Jack', he gulped, looking sick with fear, 'we're in serious trouble.'

And, two minutes later, we *both* had our trousers down.

SERIOUSLY MESSED-UP PANTS

Somewhere amidst Tim's panicked, two-minute word-vomit, I managed to decipher these vital pieces of information:

1. One of the girls in that shower room had seen our legs through one of those little skylight windows.

2. That one girl had identified us as being: one pair of purple corduroys, and one pair of poo-stained pale khakis.

3. That one girl unfortunately happened to be Sean Palmer's little sister. He has just found out. And he is pissed (in the angry sense of the word). And he is also pissed (in the drunken sense of the word). Luckily, being a boy, he pays no attention to the legwear of other boys, so has no clue who owns those incriminating trousers. However, he is now on a relentless mission to hunt down the perverted, peeping, paedophilic perpetrators with purple and poopy pantaloons.

This was the point that we decided to take our trousers off.

'Oh, yeah,' Tim added, as an afterthought. 'Also, that big hairy guy's really actually quite pissed that you want to get it on with his little sister. And now he's looking for you. And me. And James. And he's got a windscreen wiper as a weapon.'

I was lost for words. There we stood, Tim and I, in ...

'Oh, and there's some gobby cow who wants to find you so her boyfriend can make you cry.'

Threats to my life were beginning to feel like stocking fillers on Christmas morning: too many of them and they stop seeming so special.

So, yeah, there we stood, Tim and I, in a girly, joss-stick and TCP-scented bedroom, with nothing on our bottom halves, not quite sure what our next move would be.

And that's when we heard the approaching footsteps.

OUTED

Tim and I froze in panic. Before we had a chance to even begin concocting some sort of plan, the bedroom door began to open.

'Hey, Edith . . . ' began the voice. And then Iain Vinleigh's head popped in, his eyes popped out, and he ran.

'Oh my god!' he yelled through the house. 'Everybody come upstairs! You have to see this!'

Oh my shitty Jesus . . .

The two of us darted around the room like a pair of headless, trouserless chickens.

'What do we do?' shrieked Tim.

'I don't know!' I shrieked back.

Tim began pulling his trousers back on. I did the same. But then . . .

'Shit!' Tim hissed, freezing in terror.

Footsteps were storming up the stairs.

'What if that's Sean Palmer?' Tim freaked.

We couldn't put our incriminating trousers back on in front of Sean!

The trousers came off again. And then I noticed the chest of drawers.

Yes!

The footsteps were rapidly approaching.

No!

I flung open a drawer and Tim quickly cottoned on to my plan: Edith's clothes! We searched for jeans. We pulled out tops, sweaters, tights, panties, a bra ... and then the door burst open.

'It's not what it looks like!' I yelped.

CAUGHT WITH MY PANTS DOWN

Edith came to a grinding halt. She gawped at me and Tim, our trousers down, clutching her underwear. Her jaw hit the floor.

'I don't want to know,' she numbly informed me.

She did not look impressed.

'No!' I insisted. 'We were . . . '

'I don't care!' she barked, before holding the door open and adding, 'You have to get out of my room.'

'We can't!' Tim pleaded. 'We'll get our . . . '

'You need to get out of my room!' she ordered. 'Right now!'

And then came footsteps once more.

'Shit!' she whispered, before reluctantly stepping inside, closing the door behind her, then sliding a puny, bathroom-style lock into place.

There was a lock? How did we not notice the lock?!

'My dad's back!' she hissed. 'If he finds me in here with you two, with your fucking trousers down . . . !'

The footsteps drew nearer.

Edith marched over to her bedroom window and threw up the sash.

'Out,' she ordered.

What?

Tim and I both stared in disbelief, waiting for her to see sense, but that didn't happen.

'Out!' she repeated.

There was a bang on the door. Edith grabbed hold of Tim and dragged him over to her window. Knowing that resistance was futile, I kicked our trousers under her bed, then Tim and I exited through the window.

In our underpants.

STUCK

Getting out of Edith's window was nowhere near as difficult as I'd expected it to be, thanks to the flat roof of the kitchen extension directly beneath. But, getting down from *there* wasn't going to be easy. On a plus side, the back garden appeared to be completely deserted, either due to the sudden drop in temperature (chilly-willy-shrinkage was an extra little incentive to not get caught in my pants), or because everyone had rushed inside to catch the two guys in Edith's bedroom with their trousers down.

'We'll go to mine and get some different ones!' Tim suggested, as he began to shimmy down the drainpipe.

There was an ominous cracking sound.

'Tim,' I warned, 'you might want to . . .'

But it was too late. The drainpipe collapsed beneath him, shattering into dozens of brittle, plastic pieces, and sending Tim flailing to the ground with a painful THUD.

Ignoring my desperate whispers of, 'Are you OK?', Tim hobbled back and forth, clutching his backside and making strange retching noises. A minute later he was calmer, resting his hands on his knees and taking deep breaths.

'I'm OK,' he finally replied.

'Is there anything we could use as a kind of step, so I can get down from . . . '

'SHHHH!' Tim ordered, holding a finger up, as he stared, motionless, through one of the kitchen windows, then . . . 'I'll be back!'

He turned and fled, disappearing across the garden, into the darkness that had now fallen.

Seconds later, the thing that had caused him to bolt emerged from the kitchen patio doors, and stepped into the garden.

It was Em! And she was alone! No Charlie!

'Em!' I whispered down to her.

But my call was drowned out by another.

'Em!' someone else called from inside.

'James?' she squinted, peering inside. 'Why the hell are you dressed like a bear?'

'Can you film me? Please?' He handed her the video camera. 'We have to get this on camera. Apparently Jack and Edith are getting it on upstairs!'

No! What is he doing?

I heard him disappear back through the house, with a loud 'Woohoo!' but Em didn't follow. She just stood there, looking . . . *hurt.*

I think she's jealous!

I think she CARES!!

Em. My Em – she does want me, after all!!!

I was about to call back down to her, but someone else emerged from the kitchen.

'What's happening?' Sean asked excitedly.

I dropped down, flattening myself against the cold, rough tarp of the kitchen roof. I peered up just in time to see Em hand him the camera, then silently stalk away. She began heading towards a gate at the bottom of the garden.

Where does that *gate lead to?*

She suddenly changed her mind, doubled back, and left through the side gate that led to the road.

Where's she going?

Come back!

I desperately wanted to call after her, but not whilst Sean was beneath me, and I was in my pants.

Piss off! I urged him, trying desperately to master the Jedi mind trick. *JUST GO!*

It worked! He went back inside! I couldn't believe my luck!

I didn't even think twice about it. I had to catch up with Em. I got to my feet and took a running leap from the roof, praying that I would clear the stone-clad patio and land softly on the grass.

It would appear I was out of luck.

IN THE GARDEN OF
GOOD AND EVIL

To be precise, my luck lasted just long enough for me to make it safely (yet painfully) onto the dewy grass of the back garden, and *then* it ran out.

'What the *HELL* do you think you're doing?' roared a familiar voice, which came from a hulking great silhouette that was heading out of the kitchen and across the dark garden, straight towards me.

Oh, crap.

I took a step backwards.

Is that . . . ?

'I'm talking to you!' he bellowed.

It can't be.

'Come here!' he ordered, like I was some kind of dog.

I took a few more steps backwards, lost my footing and fell on my arse.

'What the hell did you just do?' he growled, looming over me, and sneering down into my terrified face.

It is! It's . . .

'Did you just jump from my daughter's *bedroom*?' demanded Letroit.

Your . . . whose bedroom?

Did you say . . . ?

What?

Daughter?

Edith is your . . .

You are Edith's dad?

YOU are Edith's DAD?????!!!!!!!!!!

Is this why Edith is so hot and cold with me? Because of what I say about you and . . .

Your mum's vagina . . .

Your mum . . . her gran . . .

MY EYE!!!

I hadn't hidden my eye from him!

A well-timed yell from upstairs suddenly distracted him.

'HEYYYYY!!!!' James drunkenly yelled from Edith's bedroom window, still in his bear costume. 'There you are, you slippery little wanker!'

I assume he was talking to me. I also assume that, at this point, he had not yet noticed Letroit standing in the shadows beside me.

'Come up here and we'll film a porno!' he continued. 'We can call it *Willy Wanker and the Cock-lick Fuctory*!'

'Right,' growled Letroit, turning on his heel and marching back inside.

'Oh, shit!' gasped James, *now* realising who it was.

I hastily grabbed my opportunity and made a run for it, straight for the side gate, straight across the front garden, straight into the street, and straight after Em.

SHORT CUTS

'You know a kid called Jack Dynamite or summit?' a bitter-faced skinhead asked, as I burst through the garden gate, nearly flattening my face on his bulging pecs.

'No, sorry,' I panted, as I swerved around him. This must be ... 'Are you—?' Like a genius, I decided not to continue to ask if he was 'Gobby Cow's boyfriend' and just assumed that if he wasn't there to kiss me, he must be there to hurt me. 'Wait, yes!' I blurted, thinking on my feet. 'He's a great big hairy guy. He's in there somewhere.'

I hit the pavement at full sprint. Part of me felt bad for leaving James behind but, well, it was mostly his fault Em was half a mile down the road in the first place, so I didn't feel *that* bad.

I could see her, but I hadn't expected her to have got as far as she had. I also hadn't expected to discover that the tip of my penis had glued itself to the inside of my boxers with dried pea-mush.

Crap!

It was well and truly welded. And no trousers = extra

wag, and extra wag made every stride feel like the skin was being ripped from my tip.

This was a hindrance I did not need. But I had to catch up with Em and find out once and for all ... *DOES she like me? Why did she storm off when she heard the stupid rumour about me and Edith? If she* does *like me, then why did she refuse me two years ago?*

And ... <u>*why do girls have to be so frickin' complicated?!!!*</u>

'Em!' I called after her, but she was too far away and I was too out of breath.

I was going to have to fight through the nob-tip-ache ache, and run. I was going to have to run like never before. I was going to have to be a peni-pain hero and put her first. I was going to have to ...

Crap!

I was going to have to hide in a hedge!

There, just around the next corner, came a large group of people, heading in my direction. They were twice as far from me than Em' was, but still I could hear their rowdy cheering and yelling. They were clearly not the sort to mess with. And definitely not the sort to go running towards in just your pea-stained undies.

But, as I crouched down on the other side of the hedge that ran the length of the adjacent park, it also occurred to me that these people were probably not the type you would choose to let a young lady encounter on a dark night, all by herself. So, like the gallant young hero that I am, I continued my pursuit, crawling behind the hedge like a seasoned pro.

Taking periodic breaks to pop my head up over my leafy

barricade, I was surprised to find that I was actually making progress. If they ever make speed-crawling an Olympic event, then I'm definitely a contender. I was only a hundred yards or so away from Em now. It wouldn't be long until I reached her. I just hoped I got there before the others did.

Head down, I powered ahead, knees stinging, palms on fire, and I didn't stop until I thought I must be almost level with her. I popped my head up over the hedge, and, to my surprise ...

'Holy Jesus! Shit! Jack!' she expleted, reeling back in heart-attack shock. 'What the hell are you doing!'

I knew that I had to clear my name as fast as I could, before the rowdy-bunch arrived, or before she decided to continue at a pace that I wouldn't be able to match.

'I've come to explain to you that nothing dodgy happened with me and Edith, and I wasn't getting naked with *her*, I was getting naked with *Tim*, because we'd been spying on some guy's penis in the school showers and then I poked myself into the girls' shower room, and then my trousers were all messy, which wasn't helped by the kids near the canal, and then my messy trousers were going to give me away, so I took them off, and Edith wasn't supposed to see and, you see, it's not dodgy at all, and it's just a big misunderstanding, and that's why I'm in my boxers right now, on my knees, in a park, talking to you.'

I finally took a breath and waited for that Hollywood moment where she pauses for a second, then throws her arms around me, and we kiss, and it starts raining on us, and we laugh like rain is the funniest thing ever, and the camera pulls back, way up into the sky, the happy song starts, and ... roll credits.

Except that's not quite what happened.

'What the *fuck*?' she asked, for some reason sounding confused and looking slightly disgusted. 'Whose penis in the shower?' she questioned, then, before I had time to answer, 'You *poked* yourself into ... Did you just say you're not wearing any trousers?'

'It's not dodgy!' I explained.

'Whatever, Jack,' she sighed, turning away and holding a hand up. 'You don't need to explain yourself to me. It's your life – you do whatever freaky shit you want to.'

'But I only want to do freaky shit with *you*!'

She frowned.

'That came out wrong,' I explained.

'Jack!' she half sighed, half growled. 'I'm fed up of being your substitute girlfriend. It's like I'm always your last resort, when you've exhausted all other possibilities. But I don't want that! I deserve more than that! I'm not just someone you can fall back on when all else fails!'

I took a moment to try and take all of that in.

'But ...' I began, trying to get a handle of where I stood with all of this. 'Does that mean you *do* like me?'

She sighed, then turned, and began to walk away.

'Go back to the party, Jack. I'm going home.'

'No! Wait!' I pleaded. 'I'm running out of hedge here!'

'Jaaack!' she half growled (... no, it was a full-on growl this time). 'This is exactly what I'm talking about!'

297

She stopped again, and turned to me, but quickly averted her eyes upwards because ...

Is she crying?

'If you really liked me, you wouldn't let a hedge stand in your way! I'm right here, Jack! I'm *right here*!'

She's right. She's SO right!

Of all the things I want in my life, she is the only thing that is actually within my reach, and I keep letting her slip through my fingers.

Well, I'm not going to let her get away. Not this time!

'Look at me,' I said gently.

She bit her lip and continued to stare up at the stars, chewing on her lip, as if trying to hold back more tears.

'Look at me,' I asked again, reassuringly.

It took a few stalled attempts, but she finally looked me in the eyes, and it broke my heart. A large tear rolled straight down her cheek and dropped off her jaw.

I've made her cry?

I hated myself. Then, not giving a shit about the approaching gang of lads, I rose from my knees, reached out a hand, and ...

'AARGHH!' I yelled, falling straight back to the ground. 'MY PENIS!'

'Bye, Jack,' I heard her say softly, and she walked away.

'No!' I yelled, crawling after her. 'You don't understand! I glued my nob with peas!'

But she mustn't have heard me, because she just kept on walking. I shoved my hand down my pants, determined to unglue myself, frantically trying to chase after her, but so not able to.

And then I saw them. I saw their faces. The lads – they had reached us, and I knew who they were. Tyler and the Pygmy Warriors were spilling around Em, surrounding her, and shit was well and truly about to happen.

THE PYGMY WAR

They had been so involved with themselves that they hadn't noticed me behind the hedge. And I'd been so involved with Em that I hadn't noticed just how close they had got. Em, on the other hand, had noticed them. And they had definitely noticed her.

'All right?' Tyler asked her, blocking her path as they swarmed around her.

'Piss off,' she muttered, as she tried to step around him.

He blocked her path again. She tried to break right, but he was already there. So, wisely, she simply turned around and started walking back towards the hedge that I was hiding behind.

Unstick, you little bastard. Unstick right now!

It was absolute agony, like someone peeling away my nob-skin with a pair of pliers, but, little by little, I was tearing myself free.

If only I had some warm water, it would unglue in a second!

The option to piss myself did cross my mind, but I knew

I'd never be able to push a pee out without accidentally pooing in my pants.

But the next words I heard gave me the incentive I needed to just grip and rip.

'My mate fancies you,' Tyler told Em, feeling the need to yell, even though he was directly behind her. 'Will you have sex with him?'

Em ignored him and kept on walking.

My penis was free, but I was fairly certain there would be blood.

'How much you charge?' Tyler asked, his gang of Pygmy Wank-faces all laughing at an over-the-top volume. 'You are a whore, ain't ya?'

That was it. Now that I was mobile I was going to put a stop to it, there and then. JackMan was to the rescue.

'Hey!' I called, as I rose up from behind the hedge.

My surprise appearance had the desired effect. Almost every single one of those little shits leapt back an entire foot, and flinched as if I'd swung a blow at each of their faces at once. But then they saw it was me. And they began to laugh. And then they saw I was in my pants. And they laughed even harder. Even Em rolled her eyes in disappointment. And then ... I didn't have a clue what I was going to do next.

'Leave her alone!' I shouted, but, unsurprisingly, they didn't do as they were told. In fact, Tyler must have still been a bit touchy about the time I said his dead dad was gay, and that other time, earlier, when I kicked him in the face, because he suddenly turned an angry red, and started shouting at me.

'My nose bled for TWENTY MINUTES, you twat!' he screamed, then, with nothing else to update me on, he lobbed a beer bottle straight at my head.

I ducked it, of course, because I'm a tall superhero and he's a Pygmy wanker, but this only seemed to enrage him even more.

'Just go, Jack,' Em suggested. 'You're not helping things.'

'Yeah!' jeered some of the Pygmy Warriors.

'Even your girlfriend don't want you!' the one called Vince laughed.

'This is your girlfriend?' asked Tyler, as if he'd just had a good idea. 'This ugly fucking ginger whore's your *girlfriend*?'

That's it . . .

'Piss off,' Em told him once more.

I didn't wait one second. I launched myself over the dense hedge that separated me from them, catching myself on a rogue branch as I toppled over it, ripping my T-shirt up the back and landing on the pavement face down.

Tyler and the Pygmy Warriors were on me in an instant. They didn't actually beat me up, like I was expecting, but they literally *jumped* on me.

'Get off him!' Em screamed.

They may be small, but there were a lot of them, and they overpowered me in a flash. They flattened me to the ground. Some sat on me, some stood on my arms. Someone poured beer over my head, and someone else pulled my boxers down to my knees.

'Get off!' Em repeated, getting nearer.

'It's OK!' I grunted, under their weight, trying to sound as casual as possible. 'I've got it covered. You go back.'

There was shouting, jeering, laughing, spluttering (that was me) but, worst of all, there was screaming. Em was screaming.

'GET OFF HIM!' she shrieked.

But it only made them laugh harder.

I had to get them off of me.

And then I had a really good, bad idea.

I'm going to shit on these wankers!

BAM! THWACK! CRACK!

Suddenly, the Pygmies were dropping like flies. Em was swinging her fists like a deranged ape! She was *fighting* them! For *me*! I wasn't going to have to poo on anyone!

And then I was free! She had saved me! I jumped to my feet. (Then I fell back down, because of that part where they pulled my shorts down.)

'Pull your pants up, Jack,' she advised, helping me to my feet.

'Did you see my ...?' I panicked, quickly covering my cowering manhood.

'I didn't see the end!' she barked impatiently.

'Good, because it doesn't count if you ...'

I broke off as I turned to see the Pygmies regrouping. They did not look happy. Tyler was rummaging through a backpack for something, and neither Em nor I felt like hanging around to find out what.

'Come on!' she ordered, grabbing my hand and jogging with me back towards Edith's.

The Pygmy Warriors were hot on our heels and, soon

enough, we discovered what exactly had been in Tyler's bag.

Something *WHOOOSHED* past my ear, causing me to jolt in shock, then a full bottle of beer exploded on the road in front of us.

They're throwing bottles of beer at us!

Our pace quickened to a sprint, and another bottle came hurtling into the back of my calf, causing my leg to momentarily buckle in agony, before smashing on the ground behind me. It was going to bruise like a bastard, but I wasn't seriously injured. I was limping, though. I was slowing us down.

We weren't far from Edith's now, but at the speed we were moving, and the rate at which they were gaining on us, we weren't going to make it in time.

'You go ahead!' I panted to Em.

'Shut up,' she replied, knowing as well as I did that without her hand to hold on to, I'd be on the ground again in a matter of seconds.

I heard the horrifying, propeller-like sound of another bottle slicing through the air, spinning towards us from behind, and I braced for impact, picturing it shattering against my skull.

'Aaaarghhhh!' wailed Em, as the bottle clipped her upper arm and span out into a bush.

'You OK?' I asked.

'Yeah,' she winced.

She hadn't even faltered.

Two more bottles exploded around our feet, and it became suddenly very apparent that they had us.

A foot hooked mine from behind, and I went tumbling to the ground.

My attacker advanced.

And then I heard the screams.

JACK SAMSONITE: THE MOVIE

EXT. WAR-RAVAGED WASTELANDS (plus housing development) — NIGHT

War cries explode though the night air as JackMan's loyal army bursts forth from the mouth of House Doom. His second in command — Mummy 'James' Bear — leads the defence.

                    MUMMY BEAR
   Attaaaaaaack!

Lady Em-A-Lot takes flight towards the safety of House Doom. JackMan raises his wounded and aching body from the cold, hard ground and watches with pride and relief as his men rally in his defence. Behind Mummy Bear charges Timmylocks, (AKA The Blond Avenger, sporting a pair of spanking clean green corduroys); a rabble of newly recruited warriors unknown to JackMan, but who move with an impressive lack of coherence and balance; and behind them storms a most unexpected ally — Seanicus Palmercus (The Farmer of Arsecus). Together they form an almighty union that will come to be known as ... The League of Insignificant Random People. And the LIRP is not alone. They have themselves a Mountain Troll of the Hairy Beast breed, who, above his head, swings the

much-coveted weapon of the gods — The Mangled
Wiper of Windscreens. And, close behind him,
storms the most vicious asset of all — a
genuine, wild, rabid, Skinhead Goblin, (mating
partner of the much feared Gobby Cow Demon)
whose war cries alone are enough to send the
Pygmy Warriors fleeing for the hills.

JackMan's attackers retreat. Mummy Bear spies
his fallen leader and races to his side.

                    MUMMY BEAR
   My Lord!

                 JACKMAN (wincing in pain)
      At ease, my friend, I am unharmed.

                    MUMMY BEAR
   You have green stuff on your penis.

                    JACKMAN
   That I do, good Bear, that I do.

                    MUMMY BEAR
   And our Lady? Is she safe?

As JackMan sheathes his green sword, he
watches Lady Em-a-lot rush towards her
maidens, who usher her into the safety of The
Garden of Fools.

JACKMAN (suspiciously)
Our Lady? Yes, Bear, she is safe.

MUMMY BEAR (cautiously)
That is good, my Lord ... My Lord? I have
something I must tell you.

JACKMAN
It can wait, Bear, for now we must fight.
And Bear? Beware the Skinhead Goblin. I
fear that, if he learns for whom he fights,
his allegiance may change.

Mummy Bear hangs his head for a moment before
advancing towards the battle, then pauses.

MUMMY BEAR
Bye, my Lord.

JACKMAN
Huh?

MUMMY BEAR
Bye!

JACKMAN
What the frick? I can't hear you!

MUMMY BEAR
Bye, JackMan. Bye.

JACKMAN (voiceover)
His words left me floundering in confusion.
Was my man to leave? In the heat of
battle? No, he did not leave. He fought
with bravery and gallant-ly ... ness.

Slow motion —

The Bear turns and charges right into the heart
of the battle, helicoptering his arms and
perfecting even the most complex manoeuvres of
the long-forgotten martial art — Deranged Nob.

Pygmy Warriors are everywhere, scampering and
leaping with cat-like agility, avoiding the
heavy blows of the LIRP. It is a one-sided
battle. The LIRP appear to be unstoppable. But
then the unexpected happens ...

BOOOOM!

The Pygmies deploy a weapon so steeped in dark
magic that it leaves JackMan in no doubt ...

JACKMAN
They have been armed by the Dark Wizard!

Their glass bombs come hurtling through the
air like magical, cold, hard, comatose,
kamikaze pigeons.

JackMan watches in horror as his men advance
towards certain bruising, definite wetness, and
possibly even cuts and scratches.

The Pygmies, now swinging in the trees,
leaping from branch to branch, whoop and
holler in their alien dialect as their bombs
explode around the feet of their enemies.
Glass shatters and the Dark Wizard's alcoholic
potion sprays out, dousing the legs of the
LIRP. Timmylocks takes evasive action,
hopping, skipping and dancing away from the
fizzy poison, but it's no use — one of the
glass pigeons explodes onto a tree trunk next
to him, and he is peppered with dampness, all
the way up to the knees of his green corduroy
fancy-pants.

JACKMAN

NOOOOOOOOO!!!!

TIMMYLOCKS

Eeeeeeeeek!

The casualties are too many. Sixty per cent of
the LIRP have fallen victim to soggy ankles,
and they know that their fight is up.

SEANICUS PALMERCUS

Run away!!!

The LIRP immediately disperse. Most retreat
into the realm of Griffith's Parkland, but a
handful head back to House Doom, the Pygmy
Warriors hot on their heels. But, as they
approach the glowing entrance to House Doom,
JackMan notices something begin to block
their route, something that begins to block
the *light,* something that JackMan fears to
be . . .

                    LETROIT THE FRENCH NAZI ZOMBIE
        Zeh party is overgh! Be gone!

                    JACKMAN
        But we seek refuge, Letroit! I bring
        smaller, incoherent, drunken warriors for
        you to feed on in return for safe passage.

                    LETROIT THE FRENCH NAZI ZOMBIE
        Ay said BE GONE! Or I shall feast upon
        your genitals! And not in a nice way!

JackMan throws up in his own mouth a little
bit, then, as the door slams in his face, he
hears the voice of a mildly slutty siren
calling to him from the side gate.

                    MAIDEN SALLY
        This way, you div! Quickly!

As I dashed through the open gate, I noticed what Sally had in her hand – the video camera. Yes, she had filmed it. The entire battle.

Our fight scene!

Our documentary-style fight scene!

OK, so maybe it didn't go down *exactly* as described above, and there were probably a few too many heroes and villains for Ben Marshall's liking, but, still, it was pretty damn awesome.

As I continued into the back garden, I was closely followed by Tim, then Sean. I turned, heading for the kitchen doors at the back, but then I noticed Em and Edith calling me from the bottom of the garden. They were holding the back gate open. I sprinted towards them, and discovered that on the other side of the gate was the canal.

'We're going to Em's!' Edith whispered loudly.

I'm not sure if this escape plan was to evade the Pygmy Warriors, or to keep the party going, but I wasn't going to stop and ask questions. We waited for the last of our soldiers to make it onto the canal path, then closed the gate, and ran on in silence. Until . . .

Shit!

'My bag!' I gasped, skidding to a halt and causing James to crash into the back of me.

He's back? What was all the 'Bye, Jack' stuff about, then?

'Forget your bag!' he ordered, running on.

'No! I left it in the kitchen!' I explained.

'It doesn't matter!' he hissed. 'Get it tomorrow!'

'No!' I repeated, trying to explain. 'It's got my *costume* in it!'

He finally stopped.

Yes, my bag, with *that* costume inside, was sitting in *Letroit*'s kitchen, just waiting for him to peek inside … waiting for him to nail me once and for all.

James thought about it for a moment, weighing up our options, before making a decision.

'Forget about it,' he said resignedly. 'He won't look inside. Come on.'

He turned and continued running. I reluctantly followed. James checked to make sure I was keeping up, then upped his pace in an attempt to catch up with the others, who hadn't even realised we'd stopped.

He was right. Why would Letroit go looking through my bag? He wouldn't. But …

What if he did?

I couldn't take that gamble.

I gradually decreased my speed, making sure James didn't hear me drop back, then, when he was a good distance away, I turned and headed back to Edith's.

I knew exactly where I'd left my bag – right by the back door, in the kitchen. All I had to do was sneak across the back garden, open the door and slip it out.

It'll be easy, I told myself.

I was wrong.

THE CAT BURGLAR

I peered through the gate at the bottom of the garden. The garden was empty. The kitchen was empty. The Pygmies must have given up. I ran for it.

As I reached the back door, my worst fear was realised – LOCKED!

Idiot! Of course it's locked!

But then I spotted the cat-flap in the bottom of the door. It wasn't big enough to fit my whole bag through, but if I could *reach* my bag, then I could at least remove the costume, and fit that through. That would be totally doable!

I got down on the cold, stone patio, reached inside and … soon realised that, contrary to my prior beliefs, my arms are not actually six feet long. My bag was *miles* away!

'Frick!' I whispered to myself.

And then I heard someone whisper a reply.

'Tilt it the other way!'

I whipped my head round to see who it was and, to my horror, saw Tyler and Vince backing out of Letroit's garden shed, carrying a step-ladder, whispering to each other, unaware of my presence. They were struggling to fit the ladder through the doorway but, once they had, they were undoubtedly going to use it to get onto the kitchen roof, and in through Edith's open window.

What are those little twats doing?

Do they think we're inside? Are they taking the war to Letroit's house? Or are they just thieving little criminals?

They hadn't noticed me, but that would only last as long as they struggled with that ladder. I slowly and silently began to slip my hand back out of the cat-flap, but, as I did so, my wrist caught on something protruding from the other side of the door ...

Something that dislodged.

Something that fell with a TING-A-LING!

The Pygmies froze. They turned. And then they saw me.

'He's got our bag!' Vince yelled.

What?

'Boys!' Tyler called out to the rest of his army, who must have been waiting out front.

And then they ran for me.

I frantically groped around on the kitchen floor, hoping to god that that 'ting-a-ling' had been what I thought it was.

Tyler and Vince were closing in on me.

I began kicking, in preparation to fend them off. My foot connected with something. A bag. *Their* bag. Their bag, still half-full of beer.

My fingers closed around a cold metallic object in the kitchen.

I yanked my hand out and uncurled my fingers.

A hidden key!

I jumped to my feet, clumsily fumbled the key into the lock, then turned ...

CLICK!

My heart leapt with relief. I turned the handle, grabbed Tyler's bag, slipped inside, then ...

Tyler and Vince piled in behind me.

I scooped my bag from the floor, then bolted for the stairs.

ESCAPING NO. 2

'Who the hell . . . ?!' I heard Letroit yell from another room, followed by his thundering footsteps.

Oh, shit! Oh, shit! Oh, shit!

'HEY!' Letroit's voice boomed from close behind, followed by a boy's yelp.

He had caught Vince, but Tyler was still on my tail; though, at this point, I imagined he was running *from* Letroit rather than *for* me.

I reached the top of the stairs, Tyler just two steps behind me. I darted straight through the nearest doorway, slammed it shut, and prayed that it had a lock.

I was in luck.

But, before I had had a chance to slide the lock into place, the door burst open, and Tyler darted in. I was squashed behind the door, so that I was completely hidden. I peered around it and watched as Tyler paused, then disappeared through another doorway, directly beside me.

I could hear Letroit still tussling with Vince downstairs, so I made my move. I shot out from behind my door, saw a panicked Tyler standing in a small en-suite bathroom, then slammed his door shut. I didn't know exactly what I planned to achieve by this, especially as the bathroom lock was on his side of the door, but then I noticed a television cabinet beside me. Carefully holding the door shut by the handle, I slid the cabinet across, in front of the outward-opening door.

Crap!

Too light. The plasma TV inside was nowhere near heavy enough to keep Tyler from getting out. But ... as I slid it into place, I realised that the cabinet was the perfect height for wedging firmly beneath the door handle, and so preventing Tyler from being able to push it down and open it.

Ha! He's trapped!

But, judging by the sound of Letroit racing upstairs, so was I.

I slammed the bedroom door shut and, this time, slid the lock into place with one second to spare.

BOOM!

The door flexed as though it was made of rubber as Letroit's oversized body slammed into the other side of it. A crack instantly appeared in the doorframe, next to the lock.

Oh, dear.

I ran straight for the window, hoping that, like Edith's window, it would open out over the kitchen roof. No such luck. I tried to open it, to see if there was *anything* below that could aid my escape, but closer inspection revealed that the sash was firmly painted shut.

A cacophony of furious door-banging was accompanied by the booming of my heart and the throbbing of my head.

'Edith?' Letroit called from the other side of the door.

He had momentarily paused in his attempt at breaking the door down, and had resorted to merely thumping it, which was good, because I wasn't sure how much longer that door would hold.

'Edith, is that you?' he growled furiously.

He hadn't seen who it was! That was good. But it wouldn't last for long if I couldn't find a way out of there.

Think! I ordered myself, *THINK!*

A knife. I needed a knife. I could cut through the paint, then open the window. I shot to the bedside table, threw open the drawers, and began searching.

There must be SOMETHING!

But, no matter how deep I searched, I found nothing of any use: socks, pants, batteries, books, reading glasses, torch ... *Anyone who keeps a torch in their bedside drawer HAS to have a penknife, too!*

This was clearly a man's room: Letroit's room. There was not one single girly thing about it: grey bed-sheets, politician-style lamps, grey curtains ... but no knife!

Come on! Everyone keeps a burglar-defence weapon beside their bed, don't they?

But not Letroit. The closest thing I found to a weapon was some bendy stick, made out of a string of balls, which I felt I didn't want to touch.

And then I remembered!

Tyler's bag! He's a little criminal: he MUST have a knife!

I threw Tyler's bag open, tipped it upside down, and the contents fell onto the floor with a loud clinks and clatterings.

'HEY!' Tyler protested from the other side of the bathroom door, obviously recognising the sound of his beer bottles.

But beer bottles were not the only thing to come out of that bag.

HOLY SHIT!

Cash – credit cards – wallets – purses ... LOTS of purses! It was full of stolen crap! I quickly delved through the contents, looking at IDs and drivers' licences. They mostly belonged to old women and old men, but a few I recognised as people from our school: Clive Cornish, the science teacher; Abi Flint, from the year below ... *this hide-and-seek-playing, food-throwing eleven year old is a fully fledged criminal! I could get so much revenge from this stuff! All I need to do is get it into the hands of the ...*

'The police are on their way!' Letroit warned me from the other side of the door.

Yes!

But then my stomach lurched, violently.

No!

I HAVE to get out of here! NOW!

I, all of a sudden, felt very ill.

I, all of a sudden, wished I hadn't locked Tyler in that bathroom, because my long-awaited crap was on its way out and there was nothing I could do to stop it.

I darted back to the window, determined to crack it open.

You can do this! It's only paint!

I gave one almighty push against the sash, and I heard the seal break ...

Except it wasn't the window seal I had cracked open.

Oh, no . . .

I'm crowning!

I froze. Unable to move.

Tyler continued to yell for release.

Letroit resumed his attempt to break the door down.

I pictured the police racing towards the scene.

And I could not move a muscle. Not without triggering a full-blown bum-explosion and giving birth to a giant poo.

I knew it was only a matter of time. I was fighting a losing battle. It was coming out, and there was nothing I could do to stop it.

A text chimed in on my broken phone. Hoping it was help on the way, I tried to read it on the barely functioning screen.

' . . .re are you?! . . . Upstairs, waiting . . . totally naked . . . with Charlie . . . '

WHAT THE FUCK???!!!

That was the final straw. My insides were coming out, and there was no stopping it.

I reached for my bag, searching for something to catch it in.

And that's when I saw it . . .

That's when I hit breaking point.

That's when I gave in.

That's when those two fateful words shot through my mind and took over my brain . . .

1. *Fuck*

2. *It.*

TWO WORDS

You see, these are not just any two words; these are the two very words that always have and always will precede every act of stupidity in the history and future of mankind. For these are not mere words, they are a state of mind. Or, to be more precise, they symbolise an *absence* of mind.

But at this moment in time, they were all I had. And, thanks to them – thanks to my absence of mind – I walked out of that house, completely unharmed, completely untouched, completely unseen ...

IN EM'S BED

As I ran, flat-out, to Em's house, I tried to retain my absence of mind. I really didn't want to think about that text message, about what it meant, about who it might have been from. But my attempts were futile. It was all I thought about all the way there.

Charlie.

It was all I thought about as I stepped through Em's open front door. It was all I thought about as I slipped past the living room full of loud, laughing voices. It was all I thought about as I crept up the stairs. And it was all I thought about as I silently turned the handle of Em's bedroom door.

Please don't let this be bad.

Please let me have a happy ending!

The bedroom was bathed in darkness. But a shaft of light cut across the room. A bright, white light.

A projector?

A torch?

A . . .

The blinking red light told me it was the light mounted

on the video camera. It was filming. But filming what? I couldn't see anyone! Just an empty bed.

I stepped forward.

I froze.

It wasn't empty. The bedcovers moved. Someone was underneath them.

Who?

One person, or two?

Is someone waiting for me, or . . . ?

I took another step closer. Something about the bed, the way the camera light shone on it, reminded me of an empty stage awaiting a show.

And a show is exactly what I got.

A leg slid out from beneath the covers.

I took a step . . .

Back.

Go back!

I felt ill again. So very ill!

The leg had hair on it. A man's leg!

No!

I heard a groan of pleasure.

My insides threatened to come out again, but this time through my mouth.

I held them in.

I took another step back.

Get out of here! Get out!

But I wasn't quick enough.

Another groan.

Another leg slipped out from the covers.

A . . .

What?

It can't be!

But the covers pulled back just enough for me to be sure of the four legs before me. And then the next groan came, only this one was in the form of a name.

'Charlie ... '

THE END

I stood there in the hall, head spinning, heart pounding, trying to make sense of what I had just seen. But it didn't make sense. No sense at all.

So much hair!

'Psst!' came a voice.

I turned.

Nobody. I was all alone.

What is going on with my head?

'PSSSST!' the voice repeated. 'Up here!'

I looked up, and there she was, head poking down from the newly converted attic.

Em.

Em!

'Don't go in there!' she warned, not speaking above a whisper.

Too late.

'Was that ...?' I began, but was unable to finish.

Em smiled and nodded, in a consoling kind of way.

'James,' she finished for me, 'and Charlie.'

James and Charlie ...

Four hairy legs ...

Charlie is a guy ...

James is gay ...

MY James is GAY?!

Why can't people surprise me with their gayness at CON-VENIENT times?!

'But ...' I stuttered, 'you told me Charlie wasn't camp!'

'You don't have to be camp to like guys, Jack,' she educated me.

'So James is ...'

JAMES IS GAY????!!!!!!

'He's been trying to tell you for weeks,' she explained softly, 'but ...'

He can't be gay. He likes girls! I KNOW he likes girls!

And then it suddenly dawned on me ... the thing that James wanted to tell me at the Pygmy Battle ... he wasn't saying '*Bye* Jack' at all ... he was saying, 'I'm ...'

James is bi?

'Are you angry?' she asked.

Angry? Was I angry?

'No!' I insisted.

I'm confused as hell, but ...

'I'm relieved!' I sighed.

'Really?' she asked, surprised.

'I thought that was ...'

I gestured back towards the bedroom, but I didn't finish.

'You thought what?'

'In there ... I thought that was ...'

A lump began to form in my throat. I couldn't speak.

'You thought it was *what*?' she demanded.

327

Not 'what' – 'who'!

I swallowed back the lump. And then I spoke.

'I thought that was ... that ... was the gayest thing I've ever seen.'

Em tried to catch the giggle that spluttered from her mouth, then she disappeared into the attic.

Why was the video camera in there? Was that the love scene for our film? We have a big fight scene! We have superheroes ... (ish). And we have a great big brilliant gay love scene!

Well, Ben *did* say to make something brave and original.

'Where the hell did you get those clothes from?' she called back. 'Did you mug a giant?'

'Kind of,' I replied, not wanting to remember the incident in Letroit's bedroom.

Letroit ...

'You could have mentioned that he's Edith's dad!'

'Who? Mr Far—? Peter? Jack, it's all anyone's been talking about all week! If you weren't so busy writing in that book all the time, maybe you'd pay more attention, and not end up insulting people's entire families to their faces!'

'Yeah, well, you never warned me that her brother was ... whatever it is he's got!' I rebutted.

Her face reappeared at the top of the stairs.

'LIC?' she smirked, raising her eyebrows. 'Yeah, I googled it after she told me her brother's training to be a teacher. It's not a mental illness at all. It stands for Low Intellectual Capacity. He's just stupid!'

'Are you being serious?' I stood there, agog. 'Why would

she make out like ... what's wrong with her? What's wrong with her entire family?'

'Are we going to talk about Edith all night or are you going to get those stupid massive clothes off?'

'Get these stupid ... *off*?' I murbled, not convinced I'd heard her correctly.

'Yes,' she confirmed. 'You're having a shower if you think you're getting anywhere near my bed tonight.'

I froze.

Anywhere near where*?*

Does she mean ...?

'I got your email.' She smiled. 'Thank you.'

'I ...'

The email ... I never did manage to ...

'Come on!'

She disappeared back into the attic.

Is this really happening?

I heard the noise of a shower being turned on, then Em's top came flying down the stairs.

Oh ...

Then her jeans.

My ...

Then her bra.

God!

'Hurry up, Jack!' she growled. 'I really want to see ...'

THE END

JACK SAMSONITE'S PERSONAL STATEMENT: FINAL DRAFT

My name is Jack Samsonite, and who I am makes no difference to you. By the time I tell you, all that information will be obsolete. People change. Good guys turn bad. Bad guys turn good. Some meet somewhere in between and blah blah blah . . .

I know I'm supposed to sum myself up in two pages, but, really? A whole life in just two pages? I can't stick to that rule. I'm no good at following orders, ticking boxes, adhering to a formula . . . I'm just not that mainstream. And my life isn't a Hollywood movie. I can't force cool things to happen, or plan when someone will kiss me, or choose how many villains will try to hurt me, or how often my penis might accidentally pop out, and then wrap it all up in a nice, neat, tidy package (my life, that is, not my penis). I am not a cellophane-wrapped, mass-marketed, supermarket product. I am organic. I am a sprawling mess. And that's how I like it. The new, sexier, cooler, more confident me can go screw himself. I don't want to do the perfect thing all my life. I want to do the strange *thing.*

So no, I can't condense myself into two pages. I can, at best, sum up TWO DAYS in this 300-page journal (with bits of screenplay included), plus a ten-minute documentary (originally intended to be a stupid superhero film), which follows three students struggling to make sense of being seventeen. These are both my personal statement and my portfolio of work. They should also explain why you received that messed-up character reference from Peter Farleigh, describing me as 'someone with no redeemable attributes whatsoever'. Watch the film, read the book, and decide for yourself if that's true. But I can assure you that, whatever judgement you make about who I am, the only thing you can be sure of is this ...

I will NEVER wear pale khaki combats again.

EPILOGUE: The Epic Log

(The chapter that I didn't really want the university to read)

JACK SAMSONITE: THE MOVIE

INT. LETROIT'S BEDROOM — DAY

It's no use. The window is sealed tight. Jack is trapped, and Letroit is moments from breaking in. Jack drops to the floor ... and that's when he sees it. Poking out of the top of his bag — the folder that Julie Quill had given him — everything he needed to apply to a university course. Including ...

'A Character Reference for Jack Samsonite.
This student has no redeemable attributes whatsoever. I could not recommend him on any level. He is youth at its worst.
Yours sincerely, Peter Farleigh.'

Cut to: -

Jack's two hands reach across to the two doors
that keep his pursuers at bay. His two hands
unlock the two locks. The bedroom and bathroom
doors burst open in perfect unison, completely
enveloping Jack in the process. Tyler bolts
directly into the grasp of Letroit's gigantic
hands. Letroit immediately begins to drag the
little trespasser out, but, as he is leaving
the room, something catches his eye —
something that looks remarkably like that
incriminating Gingerbread Man costume, poking
out of a bag — a bag full of beer and stolen
wallets, a bag with a tag, a tag with a name,
a name spelled 'TYLER'.

As he moves back into the room, inspecting the
little Pygmy peeping-tom pervert's disguise,
neither he nor the struggling Tyler notice the
Jack-shaped figure slip out from behind the
bedroom door with a borrowed change of clothes
under one arm, and then exit the room.

EXT. CANAL PATH — NIGHT

Jack crosses Letroit's back garden, exits
through the gate, and enters the freedom of
the canal path. As the sound of police sirens
ring out through the night air, a contented

smile creeps across Jack's face, and he walks
with a new-found spring in his step.

VOICEOVER
(Morgan Freeman)

I'd like to tell you that Tyler went to
jail and got expelled for his life of
crime ... but life is not that just. The
police simply put him on the young
offenders list, and the school merely made
him wear that Gingerbread outfit every
lunchtime, for four weeks, roaming the
corridors with a 'I'm a thieving pervert'
sign hung around his neck. No one believed
his protests of innocence. But why would
they?

I'd also like to tell you that Jack had
the perfect revenge lined up for Peter
'Letroit' Farleigh — that he managed to
publicly shame him, humiliate him, maybe
even cost him his job, or at least piss in
his mouthwash. But, again, life is not
that just.

All I can tell you is this — as Jack
made his way down that canal path, towards
the girl of his dreams, he had a
certain ... bounce to his step, as if a
great weight had been lifted from him. And
he smiled to himself in the knowledge
that, no matter how much people may

334

change, Peter Farleigh would have to spend
the rest of his life being a twat, being a
bully — and having a pillow that would
forever smell of Jack Samsonite's poo.

                    JACK (to camera)
The old, geeky, loser me is back. Starting
right about *nnnnnnnnnnnnnnnn* ... now.

Cue music, roll credits, fade to black.

Acknowledgements

Firstly, thank you to everyone who read my last book and helped make this book a possibility. You rock!

Thanks to ALL of my family for supporting me and saying things like: 'No I really did like it! Honest!'

Thanks to everyone at Atom for agreeing to publish this book, especially to Sam for being an editor-extraordinaire.

And to every single one of you bloggers, whose response to book one I am still blown away by. Thank you. (Especially Jo at Once Upon A Book Case and Laura/Sister Spooky for being my unfaltering book-wielding ninja generals. Every time I google myself you two are there ... okay, that sounds kind of wrong, sorry, but you know what I mean.)

Thank you to all the bookshop people and media folk who helped promote me. The development of this book was supported using public funding by the National Lottery through Arts Council England, and a special thank you goes to them for making this book possible.

And, of course, a massive thank you to _____ for being such a

_____ and for _____
when I _____. Oh how we laughed! (Please
fill in the blanks if I've forgotten to mention you. I'm very
tired. And wet. And my thighs are freezing right now. I
won't forget you again. I promise!)

About the author

What you should really know about **Tom Clempson** is that, like many of his characters, he's a loser.

There are elements of his life that *sound* cool, like he worked behind the scenes on the *Fantastic Mr Fox* film and Tim Burton's *Frankenweenie*. But the unfortunate truth is that he spent his time fumbling around and asking questions like: '*Can I go for a wee?*'

If it had been Tom's childhood ambition to grow up to be 'a little bit crap really', he would be one of the world's greatest success stories. But actually, when Tom was little he wanted to be an opera singer.

Yes, as I said – Tom is a loser. And it is this redeeming quality that makes him so appealing. Tom's story is one of inspiration to us all. Because if he can write a novel and get it published, then the potential for the rest of humanity is truly limitless.

Haven't had enough of Tom's ~~rambling~~ genius? Head to www.tomclempson.com or find him on Facebook or Twitter (@tomclempson)